I0533259

The Painted Memories

Lila Vex

Published by Lila Vex Publishing, 2024.

THE PAINTED MEMORIES

First edition. June 10, 2024.

Copyright © 2024 Lila Vex.

ISBN: 979-8990544215

Written by Lila Vex.

To my dear readers, thank you for your unwavering support, for embracing my stories, and for joining me on this literary journey. Your enthusiasm and encouragement mean the world to me. This book is dedicated to you, the ones who bring these words to life.

CHAPTER 1

T he crisp ivory envelope seemed to radiate its brilliant aura, gleaming under the warm kitchen lights. My name was inscribed in elegant calligraphy, with the embossed logo of the Caldwell Gallery embellishing the top left corner. Just looking at it made my heart thunder in my chest.

For months, I had been haunting the gallery's website, poring over every detail about their exhibitions and open calls. Getting showcased at the Caldwell was the holy grail for artists like me—a chance to have your work seen and appreciated by the city's elite collectors, critics, and connoisseurs. An opportunity to finally break through and get recognized.

My hand trembled as I scooped up the thick envelope, the weight of it almost surprising me. This was it. This was real. After years of being dismissed as just another hobbyist, starving for recognition, I was finally getting my chance at the big leagues.

A swell of pride threatened to burst in my chest. All those hours spent perfecting techniques, obsessing over compositions, and studying color theory had paid off. Someone had finally seen the spark in my work that I knew burned bright. My paintings were being validated by the most prestigious gallery in the city.

But as my finger slid under the sealed flap, a tendril of dread began snaking through the excitement. What if this was all a mistake? What if they realized they had chosen the wrong artist and wanted to retract the offer? Imposter syndrome reared its ugly head, digging its claws into the back of my mind.

You're not ready for this; it hissed. Not nearly good enough.

My throat tightened as I pulled out the crisp sheets of expensive stationery. There it was, in black and white—an official invitation to showcase my work in a solo exhibition at the Caldwell Gallery. In three months.

Three months. Ninety days to compile an entire show's worth of my best pieces. Dread coiled in the pit of my stomach as visions of my pathetic, half-finished canvases flashed before my eyes. How could I possibly create ten or twenty masterpieces in that timeframe?

The brushstrokes that once seemed so confident and inspired now glared back at me as amateurish and lacking. The vibrant colors I typically reveled in seemed garish and overdone. What had I been thinking, believing I was cut out for this level of exposure and acclaim?

My breath caught in my throat as doubts bombarded me from every angle. This had been my dream ever since I was a child—getting dappled in paint instead of finger paint. Since then, I have been striving for my entire career.

But now that it was right before me, that cynical, jaded voice whispered that I had been fooling myself all along. That I will be talented or brilliant enough to succeed at this level. My work would be mediocre at best, and I would become a laughingstock in the art world.

I slumped against the kitchen counter, the heavy stationery slipping through my trembling fingers as I warred with myself. This was my shot—possibly my only shot. If I turn it down out of fear and self-doubt, I may never get another opportunity like this again.

But if I accepted and failed—if I truly wasn't good enough—the shame and humiliation may just swallow me whole.

Steeling my resolve, I reached for the letter again, my eyes frantically drinking in the words over and over.

I couldn't allow myself to be defeated before I had even started. Not without a fight, at least.

One way or another, over the next three months, I was going to prove my worth—both to the critics and, most importantly, to myself.

Readying a canvas with grim determination, I vowed to create my greatest work yet.

The world wasn't going to know who hit it.

I left the letter and envelope behind on the kitchen counter and wandered into my studio, my footsteps heavy on the scuffed hardwood floors. This cramped, sunlit space had once been my sanctuary, the place where I could lose myself in colors and brushstrokes for hours on end. But today, it felt more like an accusation.

Unfinished canvases littered every available surface—their half-realized images taunted me with their flaws. What had I been thinking with that jarring composition? Those muddy colors were amateurish at best. And that poor attempt at human figures looked like it had been painted by a child.

I slowly turned in a circle, taking in each piece with a critical, unforgiving eye. How could this collection of mediocrity possibly become a compelling solo exhibition? These paintings weren't worthy of being hung at a roadside motel, let alone one of the most prestigious galleries in the city.

Bile rose in my throat as I realized how badly I had deceived myself over the years. All that misplaced confidence and ego, believing I was creating high art worthy of acclaim. In reality, my work was that of a hopelessly untalented amateur still banging rocks together.

With a defeated sigh, I sank into the beat-up velvet armchair in the corner, the one I had brought home from a thrift store dumpster years ago. Leaning back, I was engulfed in the stale scent of linseed oil and turpentine, a sour reminder of how much of my life had been poured into this little studio. For what? These sad, horrifically inadequate attempts at artistry?

My vision started to blur with unshed tears of humiliation and frustration. I sacrificed my singular dream for as long as I could remember. Hour after hour, year after year, I sacrificed my normal life to obsessively practice and hone my skills. Scraping together every last penny to pay for supplies, classes, and workshops, I handled rejection after rejection from gallerists and critics, always with the unshakable belief that if I just persevered, my work would eventually be recognized and validated.

But now, as my gaze scanned the pathetic canvases surrounding me, it was laughably clear that I had been chasing a ludicrous pipe dream. The Caldwell Gallery's acceptance letter burning a hole in my pocket seemed like a cruel joke by the universe. How could I possibly con them into thinking I was talented enough to showcase my work there? The second they saw the dreck I called "art," they would surely realize their grave mistake.

My chest felt hollow and cavernous as waves of self-doubt and dread washed over me. This could well be the bitter end of the road for my dreams of being a working, successful artist. With no formal portfolio to show, I would undoubtedly be forced to slink back to a mind-numbing day job—my passions forever shelved in order to pay the bills. A failure, just like my parents had predicted all those years ago.

The gnawing fear of impending failure coiled through my body, leaving me frozen on that ragged armchair, tears streaming silently down my cheeks. Maybe it would be better to just politely decline the gallery's invitation before I embarrassed myself even further. At least then I could retain a shred of dignity and self-respect.

I was pulled out of my miserable reverie by the trill of my phone's ringing. Swiping at the damp streaks on my cheeks, I glanced at the screen. It was Emma calling, surely wondering if I had received any response from the gallery yet.

A fresh pang of shame lanced through me. Emma had been my biggest supporter and champion from the very beginning. How could I possibly admit to her that, despite all her belief in me, I was an insecure fraud? That after years of talking a big game about making it as an artist, I was just a self-indulgent hobbyist destined to fail?

The phone kept ringing with an insistent buzz, drowning out my spiraling doubts for a moment. With a fortifying breath, I accepted the call.

"H-hello?" My voice came out as a pitiful croak.

"Oh my god, you already know, don't you?" Emma's excited voice exploded through the speaker. "The gallery contacted you! Spill it, missy!"

I opened and closed my mouth, grasping for the words to describe the gut-wrenching dread that had taken root in the pit of my stomach. How could I disillusion the one person who had always been in my corner?

"They... chose me," I finally managed in a hollow tone. "For a solo exhibition in three months."

There was a beat of silence on the other end. "Wait, am I hearing things right? Are you not excited about this? Hello, earth to Sophie! This is the big break you've been waiting for!"

I winced at her enthusiasm, fresh tears stinging my eyes. "I don't know if I can do it, Em. These half-finished canvases are terrible. I'm a joke of an artist who has no business being in a prestigious gallery like that."

"Oh no, you don't get to go down that rabbit hole of self-doubt!" Emma's stern voice cut through my pity-party. "Not after how hard you've worked and how badly you've wanted this chance!"

Sniffling, I gazed around at the depressingly bare walls of my studio. The evidence of my delusions of grandeur surrounded me. "But look at this stuff; it's amateur at best. What was I thinking when I called myself an artist?"

"Enough!" Emma's commanding tone sliced through my self-flagellation. "Do not start spiraling into your insecure bullshit right now, Sophie Clark. You are an incredibly talented artist, whether you can see it or not right this second. And you have been literally killing yourself, nose to grindstone, for years to make this dream happen."

Her words hung in the air, a harsh reality check against the dark cloud of self-doubt that had descended over me. She was right—I had sacrificed everything to get to this point, postponing financial stability, relationships, and any semblance of a normal life. All in service of my art and in hopes of one day breaking through with acclaimed success like this exhibition.

"We're not going to let your typical self-sabotaging fear allow you to just throw it all away."

Emma continued, her voice softening just a notch. "You need to buck up and remember that fire and drive that made you apply for this in the first place. No one works this hard and obsesses over their craft like you do without having serious artistic vision and skills."

A watery laugh bubbled up from somewhere deep within me. Trust Emma to give me the brutal truth wrapped in affection, just like always. "You're right; you're absolutely right. I can't abandon this now after everything. Not without one hell of a fight."

"That's my girl!" She crowed triumphantly. "The world had better get ready, because the amazing Sophie Clark is about to set the art scene ablaze. Just don't work yourself into the grave before your big night, okay? I need my best friend to actually live to enjoy her massive success."

I felt warmth bloom in my chest, and the fear was finally beginning to recede. "I've got you to keep me grounded, don't I? God, I love you, Em. Thank you."

"Anytime, babe. Now get your butt into that studio and show those snobby critics what true genius looks like!"

I ended the call with Emma feeling reinvigorated; my self-doubts temporarily quashed. She was absolutely right—I couldn't let fear and insecurity sabotage this huge opportunity before I had even really tried. With a steady breath, I slowly spun around to resurrect the tiny studio.

The canvases that had filled me with dread just moments earlier now seemed to buzz with renewed potential under my gaze. Those flaws and missteps I had been brutally fixating on were simply bumps along the road, natural steps in my creative process. There was nothing that couldn't be refined, revisited, or overhauled entirely as I worked towards creating my masterpieces for the gallery show.

A faint thrill of excitement began bubbling up from my core. This was my chance to go big, to pull out all the stops, and to create artwork unlike anything I had ever attempted before. No more playing it safe or holding back; it was put up or shut up time. If I was going to make an impression worthy of Caldwell's acclaim, I needed to stop doubting myself and tap into the raw, uninhibited fire that first sparked my passion for art.

Grabbing a fresh canvas, I started meticulously setting out my paints, brushes, and tools across the battered side table. With each familiar item I laid out, I could feel my artistic energy levels slowly rising again. This ritual of preparation has always centered and focused me, guiding me into that transcendent state of creative flow.

But as I stood before the clean ivory surface, my brush laden with cobalt blue, poised to make the first bold strokes, something gave me pause. I had a niggling feeling that something was off. Missing. I frowned as my eyes raked over the sunny square of windows looking out over the city's skyline, the same view that had inspired countless cityscapes and urban scenes over the years.

Normally, I would start by depicting that view, using the bustling metropolis as a jumping-off point, before embellishing and unleashing my imagination. But today, the concrete and glass held no magic and felt ho-hum and uninspired. My restless muse craved something new, something unexpected, to pull me out of my funk.

I turned and scanned the other corners of my studio, awash in the same stale familiarity. The piles of sketchbooks and reference materials, their pages dog-eared and filled with too many revisited concepts. The bizarre bric-a-brac of frozen plants, fabric swatches, and miscellaneous doodads that had been my usual still-life suspects. The same wooded trail I always hiked to find inspiration in nature. All of it felt worn out, mediocre, and lackluster.

If I was going to elevate my work to make an impact at the Caldwell show, I needed to start breaking free from my usual crutches and creative safety nets. My muse was hungering for something audacious, unorthodox, and eye-catching. A catalyst to push me out of my comfort zone and into uncharted artistic territory.

I worried with my bottom lip between my teeth and my feet rooted to the scuffed floorboards as uncertainty took hold. Going against my usual process and the methods and environments that brought me solace was daunting. What if deviating from my usual routine ended up being a terrible mistake? What if rebelling only furthered this creative drought I was trapped in?

Taking a calming breath, I firmly pushed those doubts out of my mind. Emma's words echoed back to me: I couldn't keep unconsciously sabotaging myself every time I felt afraid to take risks or veer from the path. This major show at the Caldwell Gallery was the start of my career on the line. If I truly wanted my art to shatter expectations and turn heads, I had to start by smashing through my own mental boundaries first.

With a determined set to my jaw, I stepped back from the easel and began to consider where I could seek out the shock of something fresh and unfamiliar. The clock was officially ticking—I had exactly three months to create my biggest, boldest, most impactful work yet.

No matter what weirdness or challenges lay ahead, I resolved to keep an open mind. To eschew my comfortable old haunts and routines in search of something capable of stoking the fires of my muse once again. This was my chance to become the visionary artist I always dreamed of being.

Failure was no longer an option I could entertain. It was time to pour every ounce of passion and energy into making these paintings for the Caldwell show, which were unique and jaw-dropping. I would start from scratch if I had to.

I was done playing by the rules and done living in fear. Whatever it took to make this gallery showcase a triumph, I was all in.

With a deep breath, I set up my easel and brushes, the blank canvas looming before me. The deadline for the gallery show was daunting, but I had no choice—I needed to reignite my passion by leaving my comfort zone behind.

Dipping my brush into vibrant crimson paint, I met the empty canvas head-on. No more overthinking or playing it safe. I let the strokes flow instinctively, slashing bold ribbons of color without restraint or preconceptions.

For that blissful moment, the world fell away, and I was consumed in the euphoric act of pure, unbridled creation. No filters, no rules. Just my muse wildly unleashed.

With each vivid stroke, I knew there was no turning back. For better or worse, everything in my life was about to be irreversibly upended in pursuit of this audacious showcase. And I had never felt so exhilaratingly alive.

After procuring my nourishment from Maisie, I made my way to one of the cozy alcove tables tucked beside the street-facing window. This little nook had always been my favorite spot in the cafe, with its plush velvet banquette, natural light, and prime people-watching vantage point. On many occasions, I had spent hours contentedly sketching the passing parade outside while enjoying a warm beverage or pastry.

Settling into the familiar cushions, I released a contented sigh as some of the lingering tension finally bled from my shoulders. My gaze drifted outward, absently following the rhythmic ebb and flow of foot traffic along the sidewalk. Puffy jacket-clad pedestrians rushed by with steam pluming from their coffee cups, heads down against the crisp morning chill. A knot of boisterous students clustered outside the campus library opposite, gesticulating wildly in that animated way of unguarded youth.

Putting tranquil moments, the ordinary scenes of urban routine unfolded before me like a real-life cinematic tableau. Just observing these simple vignettes without the pressure of putting pencil to paper had an oddly restorative effect on my psyche. I took another reviving sip of my cappuccino, savoring the indulgently velvety foam, and felt the last dregs of my existential dread begin to dissipate.

That's when my roving attention was suddenly, and firmly, arrested by the sight of a figure across the way. He was seated alone at one of the larger wooden tables facing the window, long legs stretched out while one hand cradled a slouchy hunter-green beanie atop a shock of tousled dark curls. Even at this distance, I was struck by an unmistakable sense of...well, something. He had an ineffable quality of easy charisma and intensity that seemed to fizz around him like an invisible force field.

As if sensing my fixated regard, his head turned almost imperceptibly in my direction. My breath hitched faintly as our eyes met and held for a suspended beat. His gaze was striking—almost uncannily so. Turbulent swirls of whiskey and jade seemed to cut right through every layer, piercing into depths I didn't even realize were visible on the surface.

A frisson rolled through me from the visceral collision of our locked stares, raising gooseflesh along the nape of my neck and making the tiny hairs prickle there. That fleeting contact carried an electric undercurrent of...? Challenge? Curiosity? Some nameless, thrilling form of communication transcended the purely physical.

Just as quickly as it had consumed me, the dizzying trance was broken as the stranger's intense stare slid away with ruminative disinterest. As if he had plucked that scintillating thread of connection between us taut for the merest breath of exploration before letting it go just as abruptly.

I remained frozen, my heart jackhammering as a confusing riot of reactions blustered through me. Who was this man with the penetrating gaze and charismatic aura? More importantly, what was it about him that had commanded such an inexplicably visceral response from me in that momentary interaction?

My thoughts whirled in a disorienting kaleidoscope of impressions— - intrigue, disquiet, the faintest tendril of something that felt suspiciously akin to exhilaration. I was transfixed despite the brevity of our spontaneous encounter, as if the air itself had momentarily grown thicker in the wake of that heated clinch of eye contact.

I dragged in a steady breath, belatedly realizing my fingers had unconsciously tightened around my coffee cup. Get a grip, I sternly chided myself, even as my gaze kept tracking back to where the scintillating stranger's silhouette cut an intriguing figure amid the coffee shop's muted backdrop.

Whoever—or whatever—he was, it was patently obvious that this morning's impromptu rendezvous with mystery had just irrevocably altered the trajectory of my day—and possibly my entire creative trajectory along with it. Because for the first time in ages, a very particular spark—one I had foolishly doubted and dismissed as forsaken—had flared to glowing life deep within me once more.

CHAPTER 2

After leaving the stifling confines of my studio, I knew I needed a change of scenery before those claustrophobic walls completely smothered my artistic spirit. Grabbing my sketchbook and worn leather satchel, I ventured out into the crisp autumn air with no particular destination in mind. I just needed to escape, clear my mind, and breathe for a little while.

My meandering steps eventually led me, as they so often did, to the cozy beacon of the Old City Grind café. Even from half a block away, the rich aromas of freshly brewed coffee and butter-drenched pastries wafted through the bustling street. An oasis of warmth and comfort amongst the concrete jungle.

I felt the tension in my shoulders beginning to uncoil as I approached the handsome brick exterior with its antique green awnings and big sunny windows. Potted mums and pumpkins adorned the entrance, lending a touch of autumnal charm that made me smile despite my inner turmoil. This place has always been my sanctuary in the city.

Pulling open the heavy wooden door, I was instantly enveloped in that delicious olfactory hug of espresso, cinnamon, nutmeg, and freshly baked bread. My overworked senses instantly began to unwind as the lively din of chatting patrons, clinking dishes, and indie folk music playing softly in the background washed over me.

"Well, well, if it isn't our favorite starving artist!"

I turned at the gentle teasing to find Maisie, the kindly owner, leaning over the antiqued oak countertop with a welcoming grin. Her gray curls were looking particularly unruly today, wisps escaping her usual messy topknot, and there were smudges of flour across her cheek and wine-red sweater. But her warm hazel eyes sparkled with genuine fondness as she regarded me.

"You know you're more than welcome to starve for free in this establishment," she continued wryly. "But I do generally prefer my customers to indulge in actual sustenance on occasion."

I chuckled, the familiar rapport instantly putting me at ease as I sidled up to the counter. "Well, in that case, I suppose I could be persuaded to sample one of your legendary morning buns. You know, for purely strategic reasons, to keep myself in your good graces."

"One of these days, I'll start charging you full price, and we'll see how often you grace us with your presence!" Maisie laughed, turning to retrieve a baked good from the tempting display case.

As she busied herself plating the still-warm pastry and pouring me a cappuccino, I surveyed the buzzing dining room with a wistful smile. Despite the lively morning crowd, there was something undeniably tranquil and unhurried about this place. A soothing respite that never failed to lower my heart rate and transport me, if only for a brief pocket of time, away from the stresses of the outside world.

Cozy tufted chairs and well-loved couches were arranged in intimate nooks, with sunlight filtering through the big windows to cast gilded pools across the polished hardwood floors. Overstuffed bookcases overflowed with aged tomes and eclectic bric-a-brac that only added to the sense of quirky, bohemian comfort. Beautiful paintings and photos by local artists adorned the exposed brick walls, their accompanying placards proudly displaying price tags for each piece.

My gaze lingered on the artwork—frames were bold and uninhibited brushwork, perspectives slightly askew, colors vibrated and daring. A pang lanced through me as my gut twisted with envy and self-doubt. Those canvases and frames were utterly brimming with inspiration and raw passion, which I so desperately craved right now for my own work.

"You've got that look again, hon."

I was startled as Maisie slid a plate and steaming mug in front of me, having returned while I was lost in melancholy observation.

Mustering a weak smile, I shrugged and pulled my sketchbook out, momentarily distracted by the cinnamon-laced aroma of my morning bun. "Sorry, I'm just...in a bit of a rut at the moment. You know how it goes."

Maisie made a soft tutting sound, giving me a look of such warmth and understanding that fresh doubts began bubbling up within me. What if she could see right through me, see that I was nothing but a talentless fraud masquerading behind sketchpads and paintbrushes?

But her expression remained open and compassionate. "These thin and come and go for artists, don't they? The most important thing is to keep putting in the work and keep stoking that creative fire, even if you have to seek out a few new sparks along the way."

Her words were like a bolt of clarity penetrating the gloomy fog swirling in my head. A new perspective, a fresh source of inspiration and stimulation—perhaps that was exactly what I needed to rekindle my artistic passion again. To not just recreate the same staid cityscapes and still-lifes that had become safe, predictable routines for me.

With a renewed sense of determination, I gave Maisie a watery smile and nodded decisively. For the first time that day, the gray cloud of hopelessness seemed to lift, allowing a beam of possibility to shine through.

Cradling my cappuccino between my palms, I slowly perused the dining room once more, letting the cozy ambiance sink into my bones as I plotted my next move. Maybe I would start by doing some uninhibited sketches of the café itself and soak in the quirkiness and character for a change.

Taking a fortifying sip of the rich, nutty coffee, I resolutely opened my sketchbook to a fresh blank page, the charcoal stick poised with newfound purpose. It was time to recapture the brave, unrestrained spirit of an artist on a mission.

"Excuse me, I couldn't help noticing your sketchbook."

The rich, smoky timbre of the voice low beside me very nearly made me jolt from my seat. I had been so engrossed in hazily replaying that molten lock of eye contact that I hadn't even registered the mysterious stranger's approach until he spoke.

My head whipped around, words of startled protest dying on my lips as I found myself pinned once more by the sheer magnetism of that whiskey-burnt stare. Up close, the intensity was utterly arresting, yet rather than feeling threatened or unnerved, an unexpected sense of thrilling anticipation bloomed in my core.

The man regarded me with open curiosity, seemingly unruffled by my wide-eyed gaping. One side of his tantalizingly full mouth had quirked ever-so-slightly, a hint of teasing amusement playing at the corners.

"You have the look of an artist about you," he continued in that molten cadence, gesturing toward the sketchbook lying ignored on the table between us. His voice carried the faintest hint of an accent I couldn't quite place, the subtle lilt and elongated vowels summoning unbidden thoughts of velvet whispers and draping silk in shadowed chambers.

I gave a stunned blink, belatedly realizing I should probably respond instead of continuing to gawk so boorishly. "I...well, yes. I am an artist, that is. Or I'm trying to be at any rate."

The self-deprecating mumble emerged before I could rein it in, that cursed spiral of self-doubt attempting to reassert its insidious hold. But the spark of interest flickering behind the smoky emerald depths of my strange coffee companion's gaze didn't dim in the slightest.

"Surely you don't doubt your talents?" His tone was gently chiding as he leaned in a degree closer, near enough for me to detect subtle notes of bergamot and spice clinging to the heated aura surrounding him. "In my experience, artists are the ones who see the world most vividly of all. Who revels in the hidden colors and perspectives the rest of us unconsciously gloss over?"

A soft, bewildered huff of laughter escaped me as the unexpected flattery washed over my senses. Who was this man who could so effortlessly disarm my typical cynicism and chronic second-guessing with but a few deftly murmured observations?

"You seem to have given this quite a bit of thought," I heard myself replying in a tone hovering between wry and genuinely intrigued. "Are you an artist as well, then?"

A look I couldn't quite decipher flickered across his striking features—gone nearly as quickly as it manifested. "Once upon a time, perhaps. These days, I merely observe and appreciate where I can."

An enigmatic response, if ever there was one. My curiosity was well and truly piqued now, all traces of shyness and self-consciousness temporarily banished. I found myself leaning in infinitesimally, unconsciously seeking to draw more of the thrumming undercurrents of mystery swirling around this captivating stranger.

"And what intriguing observations could you possibly have picked up from a ratty old sketchbook and a traumatized artist like myself?" The flirtatious lilt that crept into my tone surprised even me with its sudden appearance.

Rather than appear ruffled or off-put by my playful banter, the man's gaze only seemed to intensify further. Like a predator, both fascinated and wildly delighted to have encountered remarkably engaging prey.

"My dear, I've made a special study of the human psyche and soul. Of the innumerable sparks and forces contained therein, both bright and dark, that coalesce to inspire the greatest achievements and deepest tragedies of our kind, His voice had dropped to an intimate murmur; those words seemed to wrap around my very nerves and burrow deliciously beneath my skin.

I felt an unmistakable frisson glissade down my spine, every alarm primed to detect even the barest whiff of condescension or pomposity disarmed and rendered silent by his spellbinding tone. Rather than dismissing him as just another self-important blowhard, I found myself unmistakably hungering to hear more.

Slowly, unhurriedly, the bewitching stranger reached across the scant distance separating us to trace one long finger over the exposed edge of my sketchbook in a shockingly intimate caress. My breath caught in my throat, and I could have sworn his lips curled in a secret smile—a wolf with the scent of its latest obsession in its sights.

"In your particular case, I perceive a fiery but troubled muse. One torn between the despair of self-doubt and the intoxicating longing to escape that suppressive inner darkness." His fingertip continued stroking featherlight over the crinkling paper as he murmured the charged words. "You burn to create, but the flames have faltered, grown dim, and are guttering. You crave a spark to rekindle the smoldering embers into a proper inferno once more."

A tremulous shiver skated over my skin as the potent truth of his mystical assessment arced through me. My lips had parted on a stunned inhalation, and every nerve attenuated towards this spellbinding creature beside me. It was as if he had effortlessly seen into the very depths of my soul, laying bare the tangled, twisted thorn patch of self-doubt and artistic constipation that had entrapped me.

Who was this man, and how was he so easily unraveling all of my defenses and caustic cynicisms with nothing more than a few enigmatic murmurings?

Before I could give voice to even a single one of the dizzying swirl of questions blooming inside me, the stranger abruptly withdrew his touch and straightened in a lithe, sinuous movement. A secret, indecipherable look flickered across those chiseled features, there and gone again like a spark glinting in the impenetrable depths of the ocean at night.

Then, just as abruptly as he had appeared and enthralled me, the mysterious stranger inclined his head in a tangible farewell and turned to make his departure, a cyclone of dizzying questions and half-plucked threads of connection swirling in his inexplicable wake.

Just when I thought the strange and captivating encounter was going to end as abruptly as it began, the mysterious man paused in his departure. One booted foot hovered above the scuffed hardwood as if he had metaphorically caught himself mid-step.

A pregnant beat of silence stretched taut between us, thrumming with unrealized potential and the faintest frisson of...anticipation? Longing? I couldn't be certain, but some indefinable force seemed to crackle in the heated space separating us.

Then, slowly, the striking stranger turned back to face me once more. His expression was unreadable yet somehow softer around the edges, more open and considering than before. It was as if he had awoken to some new possibility taking shape in the ephemeral currents swirling between us.

"You'll forgive me; I don't often indulge in such..." He trailed off, his full lips quirking in an almost self-deprecating manner as his piercing gaze roamed over me in a singularly weighted look. "Pleasantries. Not anymore, at least. But you've awoken something in me. A memory, a distant ember I had believed long extinguished."

My mouth went inexplicably dry as I registered the sudden shift in his energy—that mercurial intensity dialed to inscrutable levels of simmering restraint. Despite the import behind his cryptic words, my intuition told me he wasn't referring to anything nefarious. If anything, it was as if he were choosing to unmask himself before me piece by piece by tantalizing piece.

When I remained frozen in silence, hardly daring to move or breathe for fear of shattering this spellbound suspension, the corner of the stranger's lush mouth curled in the hint of a rueful smile.

"Very well then," he continued, something of that molten timbre having returned to his cadence as he stepped forward once more. "If you'll indulge an existential vagabond who no longer subscribes to the trivialities of social inhibition..."

With that silken murmur, he folded himself into the empty chair opposite me with a startling, sinuous grace. Our knees were a mere whisper apart beneath the snug confines of the tiny bistro table, the heat of his powerful presence filling the scant space as violently as a clap of summer thunder.

Up close, the sheer intensity of his magnetism was utterly disorienting. His scent—bergamot and spice interlaced with hints of worn leather and brushed steel—surrounded me in an intoxicating cloud. My senses were utterly consumed by the proximity of this riveting stranger—that inexplicable kindling of visceral connection from before flaring to roaring life once more.

Somehow, against all logic or reason, I knew I wouldn't be dismissing this electric charge between us so easily a second time. This man wasn't going to be faded into a baffling yet inconsequential blip on my radar, no matter how strenuously my rational mind might protest.

Something profound had awoken and reached out across the cosmos to tether us in this moment. I could feel the thrumming truth of that bone deep in my marrow, even if the particulars of this transcendent force remained murkily unfurled.

For an infinite stretch, the stranger simply held my gaze with smoldering intensity, allowing my defenses and reservations to wither away beneath the scorching weight of that Bourbon-burnt stare. When at last I felt laid psychically bare and thrumming with acceptance, the ghost of a pleased smile curled his beautifully sculpted mouth.

"Tell me..." he began in a deep velvet murmur that instantly enraptured me. "What first captured your senses and awakened that spark of creative genesis? What epiphanies or moments of existential revelation called out and seduced you into the raptures of the artistic path?"

I blinked dumbly, momentarily stunned speechless by how this charismatic force of nature had so artfully subverted and redirected us down an entirely new plane of discourse. Social niceties, polite introductions, meaningless small talk—all stripped away in favor of plunging directly into an intimate psychoanalysis like breathlessly excited cohorts.

And the most bewildering realization of all? Despite my typically cynical aversion to such rampantly unrestrained philosophical musings from strangers... I didn't find myself recoiling in discomfort, even slightly. If anything, the opposite was occurring—the analytical, esoteric aspects of my intellect were alive with stimulation as if I had been traversing a cerebral desert for years only to finally encounter a metaphysical oasis.

Perhaps it was the utter conviction in his incisive regard that disarmed my usual defense mechanisms so effectively. The clear implication is that this unprecedented depravity into the human experience's most transcendent philosophical cravings and abstractions was not merely idle pontification but a plain-spoken, passionate interrogation into the most elemental underpinnings of existence itself.

Or perhaps—and increasingly more likely—it was the simple, breathtaking reality that this riveting stranger inspired an undeniable sense of resonance within me. It was as if the universe itself had shifted on some imperceptible axial tilt to align our disparate energies and set a precipitous cosmic reckoning into motion.

Either way, I knew with crystalline certainty that deflection or prevarication would be an exercise in utter futility here. This mysteriously alluring force of nature would effortlessly sweep aside any banalities or evasions with the sharpened instincts and insistent intensity of a circling apex predator.

So it was that without any further preamble, hedging, or fanfare whatsoever, the words simply tumbled forth from the very core of my being in a torrent of long-sequestered truth and unbridled passion.

"I've always been in thrall to color above all else," I heard myself confessing in a hushed yet fervid rush, as if speaking the words aloud for the very first time. "The way certain shades and hues seem to thrum with their own transcendent energies capable of spawning entire galaxies of emotion and human experience within the receptive observer."

My hand arced through the air like a sorcerer conjuring mystic forces from the ether, as if my very corporeal form was briefly possessed by living conduits channeling the euphoric reveries of my rapturous muse.

"Juxtaposition, shading, shadow interplay—these are the fundamental architectures of how I seek to evoke deeper truths from my chosen mediums. To birth portals drawing the eye inward beyond the mere physical, awakening souls to the illuminated essence burning beneath every subject's surface."

I knew then that I was well and truly ensorcelled by this spellbinding stranger's hypnotic presence. Every galvanized neuron in my consciousness seemed to be realigning and hurtling along unforeseen vectors, unlocking revelations and submerged artistic philosophies I had never managed to piece together with such lucid coherence.

Yet rather than shrink from the vulnerability of laying myself so inescapably bare, I found myself only sinking deeper into a trancelike fugue state, with each emboldened confession spilling forth. Because reflecting back at me from the turbulent depths of the stranger's fathomless gaze was not judgment or dismissal but seemingly endless wells of enraptured fascination.

And just like that, the connection between this cosmic force of nature and I solidified into an undeniable profundity of kinship. In that eternal moment, the cosmic tumbler clicked into incandescent alignment, and I knew without a shadow of uncertainty that our fates had become inexorably entwined on a path beyond the reckoning of mere mortals.

I had no idea how long we remained caught in that spiritual trance, exchanging esoteric observations and ideologies like shipwrecked survivors deliriously reconnecting after eons of seclusion. The flow of linear time itself appeared to stretch and bend to the whims of our passionate conversation, with minutes blurring into what could have been hours lost in the ether.

All I knew was that by the time a minuscule alteration in the coffee shop's ambient energy penetrated the rarefied bubble that encapsulated us, I felt profoundly altered. My perspective molted and was reassembled into something both ancient and shockingly new.

The stranger was the first to become aware of our reemergence. I watched, enthralled, as his eyelids flickered once in a lengthy blink, the lambent fires banked behind his whiskey-burnt irises appearing to lessen ever so little. Like a captivating mystic bleeding back into corporeal form after a journey to the astral worlds.

When his penetrating gaze returned to me with the same molten intensity as before, all remaining senses of unbalance or displacement melted away completely. In that instant, I realized our symbiotic alignment was complete: I was inescapably and irrevocably tied to this charismatic power from now until the conclusion of the everlasting dance.

A frantic silence appeared to descend over our little vantage point in the noisy cafe. Even the unrelenting cacophony of metropolitan white noise couldn't penetrate the intensely charged aura emanating from the narrow gaps between our bodies. My skin tingled with heightened sensitivity, as if I had become a finely tuned instrument catching up on the enigmatic vibrations emanating from the stranger's own soul.

That captivating mouth arched in the smallest of smiles as his gaze swept over me in a palpable sweep of renewed appreciation. "You burn with it, don't you?" In the silence between us, his words were a low rumbling of smoke and altar flames. "That sacred, all-consuming fire of the visionary."

Despite the cocoon of hot air that surrounded our intimate corner, a tremulous shiver ran across my bare nape. His voice caressed and sculpted those words into something like a conjuring, and it was all I could do not lean raptly forward like a befuddled acolyte receiving some portentous oracle.

Perhaps noticing my rapt attention, the smile widened slightly, drawing those big lips taut to invest his magnificent face with a euphoric knowingness bordering on profanity. He appeared to grasp that I was in a transitional region beyond all comprehension, and he fully meant to guide me through the mysterious egress into those tempting abyss unveilings.

"Yet it writhes in captivity." His voice had dropped to an octave just above subaudible tones, evoking memories of quiet conversations on ancient French beds and thrillingly nasty sacristies. "Starved for release, stifled in its quest for transcendence and unbridled awakening..."

Nothing could have prepared me for the full-body conflagration that erupted within me as a result of the eviscerating accuracy of his mystical statement. This man, this unfathomable embodiment of some elemental archetype, had penetrated every artificial veil and probed into the most vulnerable parts of my being. Awakening the spark still burning but dangerously choked down - the compulsive drive that powers every true artist's manifesto.

I must have made some unintelligible sound of astonished recognition, for his enigmatic smile grew into a gorgeous display of sublime acceptance. There could be no turning back for me now. Not since this blazing forerunner of cosmic truths revealed my profane yearnings so clearly.

The visitor leaned slowly, with ponderous but undeniable solemnity, over the tobacco-stained table that separated us. Even in the midst of the clamor that surrounded our secluded hideaway, the intensity of his gaze appeared to create a vividly defined sphere of reverberation that included only the two of us caught in this fatefully vital conversation. I could hear his every inhaled breath and smell the heady combination of his natural essence and the ghost of an exotic foreign spice.

"What if I were to tell you..." His words were a gravel-rough breath of heated promise that touched my very consciousness. "...that there is a method to break those bonds once and for all? To break the bonds that are holding back your bright potential and let the muse soar unhindered into the full, blinding peak of creative ecstasy."

My breath appeared to stall within my breast as the seismic ramifications resonated forth in surging ripples. Was this charming demigod, who talked in mystical riddles and profane disclosures, really delivering the key to rekindling my dormant artistic passion? Is there a route for irreversibly unleashing the highest, most uncontrolled manifestation of my creative truths into euphoric apotheosis?

Before I could even begin to construct a response - the mere idea felt too cataclysmic and potentially universe-altering to merit anything other than careful consideration - the stranger's probing gaze increased even more. Until I was engulfed in their scorching, all-encompassing might, like a pinned insect specimen writhing under the inevitable examination of some greater, ineffable intelligence.

"Such is my gift." His words trembled with the revelatory weight of revealing prophecy as they bloomed in that microscopic space between us. "Should you prove a receptive...and worthy...vessel to accept the transcendent illuminations fate has deigned you prepared to receive?"

I couldn't possibly grasp the mystic portents hinted at by his litany of allusive metaphors and veiled revelations. But one thing was plainly and inevitably evident...

My reality was that I had just experienced an irreversible fracture. And this mysteriously fascinating demigod creature offered to uncover a new realm of uncontrolled desire and creative enlightenment that I could not imagine.

All I had to do was reach out and accept the offered illumination in both the figurative and literal senses.

With a shuddering intake to steady my resolve, I cautiously extended a hand across the turbulent vortex of energies swirling between us. It appeared to hover in that superheated void, bearing an unfathomable weight of significance.

However, the moment the stranger's fingers curled around mine in an indescribably catalyzing grasp, every synapse in my body was sparked with the searing resonance of an unavoidable realization. It was as if the final pieces of a cosmically decreed puzzle had smashed into their predetermined alignment.

And when a beatific smile of passionate welcome spread across his changeable face, I realized...

My life would never be the same afterwards.

CHAPTER 3

"Follow me."

The low crushing of Liam call was soothing, as the sound was textured and sprinkled into my mind, it spread all through me, rousing the omnipresent inquiries. There could have been no doubt that this molten feeling I was experiencing behind the curtains of those apparently two calm words was like a thick smoke in my head and chest that was breaking between me and you.

There was no doubt left - it was nothing but the truth, and thus this gnosis was impossible to confuse. One clear, unshakable edict of unto others, making the least blunder from that supreme authority that had triggered the most destructive alignment of fates like us as unlucky times after times. In such a situation, the realization swept through me like a white-hot knife, capturing my mind with a vivid force that no one can deny or resist, like the tides turning moon into a prisoner.

The confusion about transcendence as time blurred was already there before my physical body could face the surprising implications of his summons. Attracted by the inexorable gravitational force of Liam's quiet command, just as billions of years ago, masses of heavenly matter fell in line with nature's Tao to bring about the true form of creation.

It held me spellbound, breath suspended, as the energy of our previously discovered connection could now be felt following us like a sentient, irrefutable movement. We, with our decision to embark on this journey together, gave movement to that irrepressible force. Finally, as if this energy ripening around him whispered the secrets to his accord, Liam lifted his fingers to mine in a rapturous invitation.

This simple act, albeit a display of the elemental embodiment of the god's divine grace rather than mortal pretense, already epitomizes the nimbleness and agility that were to be showcased further in his finest dance. Trying to apply the idea that his every being is composed of components formed by extremely complicated astrophysical equations, he produces this fancy version of himself for the sole purpose of crossing our paths and lending his assistance.

My focuses telescoped onto the sight of his palm, fingers slightly cupped, stretching across the chasm of reality separating us. Such a simple, innocent human affectation. And yet, in that heated instance, suffused with the palpable prospects of infinite ramifications and life-reorienting reinvention, it may as well have been the very hand of the universe itself, inviting - no, insisting—I seize its profane offer.

I could feel the visceral awareness of every molecule comprising my physical vessel as it attenuated towards that beckoning appendage extended before me. Each nerve hosted a thousand replicating queries and suppositions, scattering a miasma of anticipation laced with the faintest frissons of approaching deliverance.

Electrifying pulses thrummed up my forearm from where it had been resting quiescent mere seconds ago, arcing through the vessels and musculature in rivulets of pure potential energy. Awaiting only the most infinitesimal neurotransmission of intent to unleash their cosmic magnitude into action.

Was I hovering on the precipice of a threshold, ushering in cataclysmic upheaval and metamorphosis? Could this seemingly unassuming yet charged moment prove to be the harbinger of a subtly monumental divergence from every known path of my existence to date?

As my gaze swung between Liam's gracefully supplicant pose and the lambent fires banked behind his indecipherable stare, realizations crystallized within me with the certainty of profane awakenings. This man was far more than a mere eccentric catalyst inadvertently stumbled across in a public dining establishment. Some dormant sentience pulsed just beneath the surface of his perfect aeonic symmetry.

Even the ambient energies woven into the air surrounding him seemed to undulate with a captivating numinous resonance that beckoned and agitated with equal potency. As if the very molecules comprising our microcosmic environs were picking up the blaze of his ancient essence and responding with primordial yearning, pleading to be remade in the scorching radiance of his sublime incarnation...

With a tremulous inhale to fortify my transition from passive observer to irrefutably aligned facilitator of supernal workings, I answered the insistent decree first voiced through action. Extending my own slender fingers in reply, I allowed them to unfurl like tendril offerings before the searing corona blazing behind Liam's regard.

Finally, locked together in what could be considered the very ground of the reason we came together, Liam perused (shepherded) our pivotal event, the starting point of what could further be considered its mystical evolution. That rare but exquisite eyebrow raise and unspoken sidelong glance was enough for a hint of an impending storm, and he instantly launched into strolling—aa strolling that was light but insistent, like the tune of a lament.

"It is surprising to see you have such assurance, walking around uncertainly into the city like someone in the wild," I commented surprisingly, instantly adjusting my pace to just outside his.

And mumbling a short laugh, Liam just replied to my labored banter, saying: "Is that how you put it?" "The water remembers. Real journeys, real paths across the sea never follow a telos or end anywhere. The finite calculation is defeated by the mathematics of limitless affairs."

There was this partition full of tension that attached between us. His words were just trembling on something that carried a mystical omen and a sense of self-confidence. However, there was more to his words than a trumpet call for revolt; it contained mutinous banter that left no room for another backtalk. The focus was on the unfolding of the beat of destinies, flowing through courses of providence, instead of testing things by unproductive doubts.

Teenage rebellion is innate, so I quickly fell into a comfortable silence, choosing to follow this ambitious and charismatic leader, but I kept private notions in my head to unleash later against the weird breadcrumbs of this mysterious trail. We went on the snakelike passages flanked by narrow service ways and constricted alleys, and then the mysterious growl of the city started constitution-like as we saw the distant rumble of the ocean blurring in your smothering sound.

I feel as though the first germ of hesitation began to sprout at the boundary of my mind, implying that Liam's inborn intuition might have misled us all at the same time. However, we saw the hill from a distance, which was bestowed upon us with an abundance of garbage. After the detrimental changes in the city landscape, where trashed warehousing and industrial disasters were covered, the battle started over. I could not let the chance about jokily continuing, losing a sense of humor.

"Please tell me you're not leading me into some urban re-wilding exhibition." I cast him a sardonic sidelong look, fighting a grin. "I'm not sure these shambolic ruins are what I had in mind for artistic inspiration."

Liam's lips twitched with the faintest ghost of a smirk, his piercing gaze remaining locked onto some invisible waypoint ahead. "Just shatter the mortal kaleidoscope and drink in the harmonics, little Sybil. The veils will be unmade soon enough."

Before I could formulate a sufficiently biting rejoinder, the subterranean Fresnel of ancient resonance surged through me in a shock wave of searing epiphanies and illumination. It was as if the very atomic matrices of my existence had aligned with some ultraviolet stratum of perception, suddenly able to sense the telluric harmonics thrumming from a mystic confluence point dead ahead.

With a subtle widening of his pace conveying fated certitude, Liam forged ahead down the beckoning terminus of this hidden leyline. I fell into obedient lockstep, my initial urge towards acerbic skepticism utterly consumed by the exhilarating frisson of crescendoing revelation.

We passed through a crumbling industrial archway into a cavernous courtyard choked with a riotous tangle of lilac, foxglove, and peppery viriditas. Yet the further I allowed my reawakened meta-senses to plunge into the verdant heart of this hidden sanctum, the deeper the tsunami of epiphanies and marvels crested around me.

This wasn't merely an anonymous greenspace co-opted by nature to reclaim a bombed corner of the urban wild. It was a blastosphere of Mother Earth's defiant perseverance—a living, transcendent attestation to the underlying mystery and inexorable continuum that mankind's arrogant disintegrations could never occlude.

I found myself grinning like an awestruck child, with every giddy exhale unleashing peals of pure, uncomplicated euphoria into the sanctified space around us. As Liam paused at the fringe of this locus, I spun in place, greedily drinking in the ephemeral harmonics and fractal tessellations emanating from every arcing branch and wild bloom.

"My god..." The reverent murmur of stunned astonishment fell from my lips while I shook my head in wonder. "This place is..."

"Beyond the profane adjective?" Liam supplied, his tone a low rumble of profound gratification as he watched my uninhibited reaction with undisguised approval.

Meeting his steady regard, my elated smile somehow intensified even further at the answering spark blazing behind the molten depths of his hypnotic stare. In that electric moment of reconnection, every final vestige of doubt or uncertainty dissolved into the sanctifying ether for good.

The solitary oasis, the garden sanctuary, seemed more like a catalyst for my mental and artistic fatigue for many months. Even the most persistent feelings of self-doubt and artistic frustration disappeared like a miasma (a disease-causing cloud) as we proceeded. The unique vibe of this place was as inexplicable as the quality of the air itself, which was supported physically and psychologically in the sense that it carried ionizing particles that disseminated the polluted psychic residue and deposited the crystal vitality energy.

"You can actually feel it pulsating inside you, eyes wide with alacrity, no?" Liam's husky mean uttering seemed to be mingled in a wild mix with the antiquity of the earth itself as he was about to dizzy me slightly ahead of him. "An unleashing of inspiration and unhindered creativity training?"

I sucked in the air with an open-mouthed gasp that brought that blooming, fragrant sweetness in and the mystic spiritual atmosphere close. "No way." I kept my voice down, letting my hand wander through the soft petals and their greenery on the way to where we were heading. "A symphony of atoms that had once conveyed the dancing, primordial trickle of their birth."

With a twirl, I stop and gaze at the full, bigger scene, which is simply breathtaking. How could I possibly object to that description? "A terrarium with some wild flowers" does not count as a description of a very inspiring place for me.

Liam gave me a sardonic grin behind one hefty shoulder, his eyes aiming fire at as if of a suppressed brimstone. This kind of point of view behind the unknown nature is legitimate only to a finite human mind, which cannot go beyond the impassive facade, but it surely lacks the true wonder hidden behind it, he concluded in a tone of affected disdain mixed with a wry resentment.

"So, remember, when you decided to elope to the unexplored wilderness with the shallowest artist I have ever encountered, that is what you should have assumed." I snapped in a voice imitating an outraged feeling. Stooping down, I picked up a wilted flower and, for drama, made a grand show of holding it and pretending to frown. "Am

I refined enough to fairly weigh the identity-revealing depth of another being...originating from a flower bed?"

Liam explosively laughed at my mockery with a hearty bark that reverberated throughout the temple. "Goblin! Fool around as much as you want to, comrade. But now, as I'm about to unveil, the sublime veil of the muse is for you to savor, and the highest form of gratitude will be what surprises us."

"Well, my muses are more like drowned in mud instead of buried in comma for now," I returned the words with humor running down my cheek like the bubbling water from the tap, but irony was boring and dull, so I felt better than that. It was as if the sap of a thousand-year-old wisdom tree was spiraling into me. The longer I chose to linger in this paradise, the more a monster of regeneration and a heavenly rapture first dowsed and then took over my very flesh.

Liam, not being the one, seemed to sense the impending change, and while unaffected by my growing consciousness, he floated close enough to be able to penetrate my freshly heightened awareness with his heated presence. "Come, sweet little Sybil! Let your bonds be unshackled." He whispered this softly in that smokey, smokey-vibrant, and husky voice that made me feel his breath entering my soul. "Develop into a tube that is used to charge the spiritual frequencies, which should be until free flow." 0 Use our essay-writing service to save time and ensure error-free, professional work

I found myself unable to shut my eyes as the sound vibrations of his voice bypassed all four receptors, travelled further, and tuned into my more ignited meridians that were now blazing into my conscience. The words "psychic calcification" actually made me feel the chokehold mental block imagine itself around my creations, like sock-encountering geckos exposed to the untangling grip of gravity.

As if plunged into a pool of water, I shut my eyes and swam to and fro against an invisible resistance with all my strength to give myself time to think. Then, moved by both instinct and knowledge, I turned my back on Liam and proceeded to take in the commune of guardian angels around us. My growth in sight intensified with the drawing breath at every moment, tunneling outward until my sense of absolute awareness was completely filled up with the dizzying world that was the juicy greenery and dilated buds from all the plants and wild flowers.

And at this moment, no feeling could more clearly articulate the depths and beauty of this place. This is when, for the first time, it felt like this place pulled me apart.

I hadn't stumbled upon a mere hidden garden or overgrown courtyard. This was a living masterwork of Mother Nature's most sacred design—a dynamically interweaving cosmology of primal essences and fractal abundances catalyzed into a numinous blending of fecundity and creative orgone that simply defied mortal linguistic reductivism.

My hand began to tremble at my sides as tears of rapturous epiphany blurred my vision, and the first osmotic threads of artistic passion ignited within me once more. Electricity crackled through my nerve endings like I had been resuscitated from a long sojourn of sputtering half-life back into the searing radiance of actualized being.

A heavy exhalation of pent frustration and choking miasma gusted from my lips in a prolonged rush, immediately replaced by a revitalizing draught of this sacred demesne's intoxicating ambrosia. Every part of my starving creative essence was drinking deeply, gorging itself on the inarticulable beatitudes, and transmitting galactic lore pouring from the infinite wellspring encompassing us.

I laid down my palms and cheeks upon the cool, velvety bark of the gnarled trunk nearest to me, my whole entity now conjoined in pulsations with the gently brewing source currents embodying my meditative axis of the world. As mentioned earlier, the above is the below; the key principle of the ancients vibrated among my cells, turning me into a clean vessel of many virescent influences once again.

Burying my face in the crook of his neck, the feeling of my soul reinvigorating flashed behind my eyelids, which multiplied the power of my ecstasy, and I had to tear the happy-crazy tears off my face from streaming down my cheeks at that junction. Such heightened emotions throughout the process of rebirth, to me, suggested that these authentic transformations were more than mere fantasies witnessed by the out-of-this-world media; they could be tangibly experienced, compared to the sterile review of detached media broadcast and print, the clamor of the street, the shifting of neighborhoods, or face-to-face encounters.

For a single beat of my heart, Liam and I embraced the flow state—two distinctive rainbow colors of the essence that nonetheless vibrated as a single colony-shaped cell, humming to the common resounding harmonics of some celestial anthem of heavenly orchestral music.

During this time, my mind rekindled a rich symphony of all my precious memories, like the closing of a musical masterpiece when the sounds fade away in a crescendo. However, it was unlike a blissful trance to suddenly hear the crisp sound of the battered satchel on my torso.

My fingers quivered in a clammy sweaty fever as I frantically reached into the dark depths for a faded sketchbook and, worst of all, an obscure selection of pencils, the very ends of which almost glowed with bright magical blue-white sparks of pure creative source, and I made to use them to leave the half-visible drawings as my gift to the Ancestors.

However, I only say this with the clarification that, after a long while, I got reborn to the top of the fertile era of my life from the inferior stage of the abrogation that was binding down my soul. Hark! As the muses, my muses opened full bloom in the dynastic roost of knowledge, with every orifice, artery, and vein wide open for the drenched aeration of the epiphanic inspirations, this haunted ground was offering for their reception.

Around me, the fractal patterns and sacred geometries I had been blind to even minutes ago came into prismatic focus at last. Each unfurled curlicue of budding verdure glowed incandescent with transmitted cosmological wisdoms, while every vista danced with the vivacious rhythms and shamanic numerologies of life's endlessly unspooling emanations.

I was awash, alight, and transported into a state of adulated plenipotentiaries—simultaneously annihilated and reconfigured as the highest embodied expression of the creative source crying out for manifestation through me.

As we spent more time together in the garden's tranquil cocoon, Liam and I fell into a comfortable rapport, trading stories and philosophies. I found myself drawn to his intensity and the sense that he could peer into my soul's deepest depths.

"Art is a means of expressing the inexpressible," he said, leaning back on the stone bench. "A way to capture emotions and experiences that words alone cannot convey."

I nodded, enthralled. "Exactly. It's like trying to share a dream—the feelings are so visceral, but translating them into language loses something essential."

"Precisely." Liam's eyes shone with passion. "That's why great art has the power to move us so profoundly. It bypasses the intellect and speaks straight to the core of our being."

We sat in contemplative silence for a moment, surrounded by the gentle sounds of nature—chirping birds, rustling leaves, and the soft trickle of the garden's fountain. I felt a sense of peace and connection I hadn't experienced in years.

"Do you ever feel like you're just a conduit?" I asked eventually. "That the inspiration flows through you from some greater source, and you're just the vessel giving it form?"

Liam smiled knowingly. "All the time. The truly transcendent works never feel like they originate from my conscious mind. It's more like, I tap into a universal wellspring and ride the currents wherever they take me."

"Yes!" I sat upright, electric with recognition. "It's like being possessed by the muse. The art shapes itself; you're just along for the ecstatic journey."

"We creators are merely open channels for the divine inspiration to manifest," he agreed with a solemn nod. "Our role is to remain receptive and get out of the way."

I had encountered a few kindred spirits who understood this sacred experience of the creative process. In that moment, I felt like Liam and I operated on the same rarified frequency, tuned into dimensions most people never perceive.

"You get it," I said simply, unable to mask my wonderment at finding such a profound connection. "Truly get it."

Liam held my gaze with those fathomless eyes. "As do you, my friend. As do you."

We spent several more hours trading insights and backstories, finding so many shared perspectives and uncanny parallels in our creative journeys. The sun began its descent, bathing the garden in golden hues, but neither of us seemed to notice the passage of time.

Eventually, my phone buzzed with the first of several reminders that I needed to head home soon. I felt a pang of disappointment that our magical interlude was ending, but also a burgeoning sense of gratitude and excitement.

In Liam, I realized I had found an artistic confidante and a well of inspiration. A travel companion for exploring the fertile landscapes of imagination. Someone who could help reignite my creative spark and give form to the swirling visions struggling to burst forth.

As we exchanged farewells, I felt a renewed sense of purpose and possibility coursing through my veins. My artistic rebirth had begun to blossom.

One afternoon, Liam called and asked if I was free. Since I wasn't doing anything, I agreed to meet him. As we sat in contemplative silence amid the fragrant blooms, Liam reached out and tenderly brushed stray hair from my face. A frisson of undeniable electricity sparked between us in that ephemeral moment of connection.

My breath caught in my throat as his fingertips grazed my skin. Liam's touch sent a shiver cascading through my body, awash in a tingle of arousal and longing I hadn't felt in years. Our eyes locked, and the world around us seemed to fall away until all that remained were his fathomless depths.

"You're so beautiful," he murmured, his voice low and husky. "An exquisite muse."

I felt myself leaning towards him, drawn in by some unseen force. His sculpted lips, slightly parted, beckoned to me. The scent of his cologne—rich sandalwood with hints of citrus and spice—entered me like an intoxicating cloud.

My heart raced as the charged tension built. I couldn't tell if seconds or eons were passing in his powerful gaze. Part of me hungered to devour his mouth with searing kisses and quench the yearning that coursed through my veins.

But another part felt utterly vulnerable, exposed to the rawest depths of my soul by his piercing perception. I feared he could see too much—the insecurities, doubts, and past wounds I struggled to conceal.

With a slight shake of his head, Liam seemed to rein in the smoldering intensity. He flashed that crooked, dimpled smile that could disarm nations.

"Forgive me," he said smoothly, leaning back on the bench. "You inspire such... passion. It's overwhelming at times."

I let out a shuddering breath, still quivering from the charged tension and narrowly averted intimacy. Did I imagine the regret flickering across his features, the faintest downturn of those full lips?

"No need," I managed in a slightly strangled tone. "I understand completely."

We sat in silence for a long moment, the only sounds being the rustling leaves and my hammering pulse struggling to return to normalcy. The perfumed garden surrounding us felt simultaneously like a safe haven and an erotic web, ensnaring us both.

When we finally spoke again, the conversation remained cautious, with sweeping philosophical musings and reflections on art and the creative process. But that molten, unresolved undercurrent throbbed between us, running like a subterranean riptide navigated with equal parts longing and restraint.

A low rumble emanated from deep within Liam's chest as my fingers grazed his stubbled skin. His eyes smoldered with a banked intensity, his pupils dilating until only a thin ring of green iris remained.

"We're treading dangerous ground," he murmured, his voice a deep, gravelly caress.

"I'm not afraid," I whispered, though my thundering pulse belied those words.

Liam regarded me with a look that seemed to scorch into my very essence. "You should be."

My hand stilled, hovering just above the thrum of his racing heartbeat. Was he warning me away or challenging me to breach the final boundaries?

Making my decision, I leaned in until our foreheads pressed together. I could feel the warmth of his skin and smell the heady blend of his natural musk and lingering traces of cologne. My eyelids fluttered closed as our mingled breaths intertwined.

"Show me the danger," I breathed against his lips.

A tremor shuddered through Liam's powerful frame. Then his mouth crashed into mine with unleashed fervor, instantly obliterating any remaining barriers.

His kiss was scorching and ravening, igniting every nerve-ending until I burned from the inside out. Our tongues battled for dominance in a primal duel as I knotted my fingers into his tousled chestnut locks.

Liam's hand roamed with equal hunger, simultaneously claiming and mapping every curve as if committing me to sacred memory. When he finally tore his lips from mine, searing a path of smoldering kisses along my neck, a shameless keen escaped my parted lips.

"Magnificent," he growled against the thrum of my racing pulse. "My darkest muse."

Sinking into the sensual haze, I surrendered to his artful assault. My fingers raked down the columns of his back as he pressed me into the soft grass, pinning me beneath the exquisite weight of his frame.

Somewhere in the recesses of my consciousness, a part of me marveled at the jarring metamorphosis. How I'd gone from a wilted husk, creatively and erotically starved, to an ecstatic acolyte writhing at the feet of this brooding shaman.

As Liam trailed a molten path lower, I arched against him with shameless abandon. In his heated worship, I felt reborn - a dormant part of my soul flaring to rapturous life.

This wasn't merely carnality. This was the raw channeling of pure creative energy; the kundalini-fire blazing through my awakened vessel. Every touch, every breath, and every soulful murmur stoked the searing currents until I burned from the inside out.

"Yes." I hissed in strangled ecstasy. "Unmake me, so I might be remade anew."

CHAPTER 4

I woke up to the first light of dawn peeking through the sheer curtains, my body still tingling from the passionate love Liam and I had shared just a few hours ago.

But as I slowly came to my senses, I realized something was off. Liam was shaking beside me, and his muscles tensed up like he was ready to snap. A deep, guttural groan rumbled from his chest, and it made the hair on my arms stand up straight.

I rolled over to face him and put my hand on his back, trying to comfort him, but his skin was burning hot to the touch. "Liam?" I whispered, starting to feel uneasy. "Is everything okay?"

He just let out a choked whimper that sent a chill down my spine. I'd never seen him look so terrified before - even when we were at our most vulnerable, I always felt like there were parts of himself he kept hidden away.

But now, it was like a dam had burst. His face was twisted up in a nightmare's grip, his brow furrowed, and his jaw clenched so tight that I thought it might break. His neck and face were flushed red, and his back arched at an unnatural angle, his whole body jerking like he was being attacked by some invisible force.

"Liam!" I shouted, grabbing his shoulders and shaking him as panic started to set in.

Suddenly, his eyes snapped open, but instead of the warm green I loved so much, they were pitch black, filled with a kind of despair I'd never seen before. He let out an animalistic scream that made every nerve in my body feel like it had been rubbed raw.

Before I could do anything, Liam sat bolt upright, his arms flailing so violently that he knocked me right off the bed. I landed in a tangle of sheets, choking on the taste of fear that hung thick in the air.

I looked up at Liam, my heart pounding out of my chest. He was already on his feet, his entire body coiled tight like a snake about to strike. His eyes were bulging, still filled with those shards of madness.

"Liam..." I croaked, my voice hoarse from fear. "It's me. You're safe. It was just a dream."

At the sound of my voice, he flinched. A shudder ran through his naked body, and finally, his eyes cleared, the haunted emptiness replaced by the green I knew so well. Realization crashed over his face like a wave.

"Sophia?" His voice was rough, like gravel. "Oh god, I didn't... I would never..."

The raw pain in his voice cut me like a knife. Here was a man completely shattered - the same one who usually seemed so confident and powerful, now utterly broken.

In that moment, I realized I was standing on the edge of some deep, dark pit that Liam was always teetering on the brink of. Something that could reduce this unshakable force to a shell of himself, running on pure instinct.

As he crumpled to the floor, hot tears streaming down his face, I felt my own fear melt into a kind of aching sadness. All I wanted was to reach out and protect him from whatever demons were tearing him apart from the inside.

But would he even let me in? Or would he just retreat back behind the walls he'd built long before I came into his life?

I could only hope that I'd proven myself worthy of following him into that darkness. Of helping him fight off the monsters that were always clawing at his soul.

A few days after I saw Liam's scary night terror, we were hanging out in his studio, surrounded by a bunch of new canvases and half-finished paintings. The bright colors and bold brushstrokes seemed to practically scream with raw emotion.

"I'm blown away by how you capture the human experience so vividly," I said softly, running my fingers along the rough edges of one particularly painful-looking piece. "The hurt and sadness feel so real. Like the paint itself is giving shape to someone's broken heart crying out."

Liam looked at me with an unreadable expression, his green eyes as mysterious as ever. For a long moment, I thought he might just brush off my comment with one of his usual vague responses.

But then something flickered across his chiseled face. His usual intensity seemed to fade away, leaving an unexpected vulnerability in its place.

"You're not wrong," he said finally in a low voice, running a hand through his messy brown hair. "That's exactly what I'm trying to express. To channel the darkest depths of grief and loss into something meaningful."

I found myself leaning in closer, completely captivated by this brief moment of openness from this eternally guarded man. "You've been through some really tough stuff, haven't you?" I asked softly, recognizing the deep pain swirling behind his intense gaze.

Liam's jaw tightened almost imperceptibly as he seemed to wrestle with some inner struggle. Finally, he let out a shaky breath and turned away, busying himself with splattering fresh paint across a blank canvas with aggressive strokes.

"More than you could imagine, love," he said in a rough whisper, not meeting my eyes. "Depths of pain no one should ever have to go through."

My heart ached at the raw hurt in his voice, so different from his usual steady tone. In that moment, I wanted nothing more than to reach out and soothe whatever emotional scars were still bleeding inside this proud, strong man. To draw out the poison from the darkness eating away at him from the inside.

Instead, I just waited with bated breath as the seconds ticked by. Finally, Liam's harsh brushstrokes slowed to a stop, and his shoulders slumped slightly.

"I won't burden you with all the gory details," he said hoarsely without turning around, almost like he was talking to the painting itself. "Just know that the seeming torture I show in my work comes from the most intense pain I've been through and may never fully get rid of."

My throat tightened at the devastating implication—that Liam carried emotional wounds so deep that even his searing art couldn't fully exorcise his demons.

Part of me desperately wanted to dig deeper, to keep gently chipping away until he finally shared those tantalizing, hidden ghosts. But something in the stiff set of his shoulders made me think twice about pushing too hard, too fast.

So instead, I just put my hand on his trembling back, letting the solid warmth of my touch offer silent comfort instead of words.

For a brief moment, Liam seemed to melt slightly into my supportive touch, soaking up the unspoken reassurance. But all too quickly, that hint of openness hardened as his walls slammed back down.

"I've said too much," he said tersely, abruptly shrugging off my hand and turning back to face me with shuttered green eyes. "You'll have to forgive me, love. Today's inspiration has left me."

With that blunt dismissal hanging in the air between us, Liam brushed past me in a swirl of brooding intensity. I could only watch him walk away with a strange sense of emptiness, knowing he'd let me see the tiniest glimpse behind that imposing fortress—only to let those steel walls crash shut once more.

In the days after Liam abruptly shut me out again, I couldn't stop thinking about the conflicting sides of him I'd seen.

On one hand, there was the way he'd dismissed my attempts to understand his clearly troubled past—that deep-rooted need to keep his innermost vulnerabilities hidden away.

But on the other hand, that brief glimpse I'd caught of those raw, painful scars had left me obsessed. As fleeting as it was, Liam's honesty in that moment had been so real, so haunting, that it kept echoing in my mind.

Maybe that constant echo came from my own hunger for authenticity. For someone to just unapologetically lay bare their true self without any pretense or fakeness. To strip themselves emotionally naked and have the guts to stay open despite how vulnerable it made them.

Or maybe it was the deeper sense of empathy that had been unlocked in my own heart—the urge to witness someone else's pain so I could try to ease some of the invisible weight they carried.

Whatever the reason, I couldn't stop thinking about the mystery of Liam's broken, haunted self. About trying to piece together the tragic puzzle that made up his fractured mind.

I finally picked up a paintbrush, needing to get the mental ghosts haunting me out onto the canvas. I started swirling deep blue and indigo— - vast pools of sadness that seemed to pull the viewer into unfathomably deep, lonely waters.

But I slashed ribbons of red across the blue depths at sharp angles, like soul wounds endlessly dripping blood. I added streaks of black circling the red gashes, like starless voids ready to swallow any light trying to break through.

As I painted, bits and pieces of memories and half-formed guesses about Liam's mysterious history started to take shape in my mind.

I remembered how his eyes had automatically gone to an old photo tucked into his mirror one morning as he got dressed—the faded picture showing a much younger, happier Liam holding a cherubic baby, his face almost unrecognizable with the pure joy and love shining out of him.

That terrifying nightmare he'd woken up from in a cold sweat, eyes wild with chaos, seemed so opposite to the man frozen in that distant photo. Like some catastrophic loss, he hollowed out every bit of light and life in him until he became a shell of his former self, haunted and worn down.

I thought too of the time he'd casually mentioned being married long ago, almost wistfully, but so vaguely that it was impossible to know more.

And then there was the stray poem of his I'd found while going through Liam's messy desk one day. The first line said:

"Souls buried in sunless depths, Agony's midnight is their only currency."

The rest of the words had faded into blurry smudges, but the sheer darkness of those opening lines still sent an icy chill through me.

With each layer of paint and frenzied stroke, my suspicions seemed to solidify. At some point in his secret past, some earth-shattering trauma had shattered Liam to his core—a Pandora's box of nightmares unleashed, leaving him a hollowed-out ghost of who he used to be.

Maybe the specters of grief and loss had lived in his shadow for so long that he no longer knew how to break free from their icy grip. Those protective walls of mystery were his only shield against forces that threatened to overwhelm the tiny spark of self still flickering inside his ravaged shell.

Several days after completing the anguished, haunting portrait I'd channeled from my swirling thoughts about Liam, I could no longer contain the maelstrom of turmoil.

I sought him out in the dimly lit recesses of his studio, brushstrokes splayed in manic disarray across a dozen half-finished canvases. His broad back was turned towards me, shoulders hunched with familiar intensity as he dabbed feverish swirls of crimson across the latest panel.

"Liam," I said, the sound of my own voice seeming to pierce the cloistered cocoon. "We need to talk."

He went rigid at the interruption, his arm stilling mid-stroke. For an endless stretch, the only sound was our mingled breaths, his emerging in a slow, controlled rasp.

Finally, he turned to face me, his green eyes shining beneath messy sweeps of dark hair. "Oh, really?" he murmured in that deep, gravelly voice that always made me shiver. "And what exactly do you think we need to talk about?"

I steadied myself against the closed-off, indifferent look on his face, knowing it was just a shield he used to protect himself. "Your past," I said simply. "The things haunting you so deeply that you can't help but pour them into your art."

Liam's jaw tightened just a bit, the only small sign that my words had hit home. "You know I don't like digging up ancient history; that's better left buried."

"Yeah, you've made it crystal clear that you hate opening up." I pushed back, refusing to give up. "But this wall of secrets around you is getting impossible to break through, Liam. I need—I deserve—to understand what consumes you so completely."

His gaze drilled into me with an intensity that could melt steel, his green eyes flaring up like wildfire. I braced myself for the inevitable brush-off or biting comeback.

What I wasn't ready for was the eerie way the tension suddenly drained out of his muscular frame, his shoulders slumping like all the fight had gone out of him. Liam's next breath came out as a ragged, haunted rasp that made the hair on the back of my neck stand up.

"You want to cut me open and dig out the nightmares hiding inside, is that it?" His gravelly voice seemed to echo from some bottomless pit, chilling me to the bone. "Fine then, love. You've earned that awful intimacy by being so damn stubborn."

I could only stare, barely breathing, as Liam's burning gaze turned distant and inward-looking. When he finally spoke again, the words poured out in a jumbled stream-of-consciousness flood:

"There was a woman, you see—the most blindingly bright ray of light that this world ever saw fit to bless a wreck like me with. More brilliant than any dream I ever hoped to capture with this measly paintbrush. And a child—a tiny angel whose eyes alone held more depth than all the poetry or art I'll ever hope to create."

Liam's voice cracked, his face twisting in a silent agony you could only see in the tremors ripping through his body. I instinctively reached out a hand, suddenly terrified that he was about to shatter into a million pieces from the inside out.

"Torn away," he ground out in a shredded whisper. "Stolen in the cruelest theft from a hollow, worthless shell like me who never deserved to be graced with them in the first place. One careless moment was all it took to swallow that blinding light into the black hole of oblivion."

Anguished tears streamed down the craggy lines of Liam's face, somehow making him even more heartbreakingly beautiful in his broken devastation. I kept my hand hovering, respecting the invisible plea for space, for distance from any potential comfort that might drag him back from the edge he was teetering on.

"After that world-ending loss, I went on a relentless mission to snuff out whatever feeble spark was still flickering in the empty husk left behind," he went on in a numb monotone. "Drinking and self-destruction in all their endless forms became my only charms against facing the gaping void of grief, always threatening to swallow me whole."

A shudder racked Liam's body as his scorched voice seemed to peel away the final layers of burnt pretense. "Only when the toxic haze finally cleared could I see what shattered bits of humanity were still left in the ashes of that annihilation. Only then could I gather them up...and start to rebuild some hollow version of the man I am now."

As the final haunting words faded, that ashen, shattered portrait froze in place—all the masks ripped away until only raw, ravaged emptiness remained.

Liam's green eyes finally flickered back to the present, seeming to crumple under the harsh realization of the depths he'd unleashed into the air between us. His mouth worked without sound as a visible tremor set in, the once unshakable man seeming to collapse inward.

I stood there paralyzed for a second before instinct kicked in. I wrapped my arms around his shaking frame, holding him tight as the tears he'd held back for decades finally burst free in gut-wrenching sobs.

I succumbed to the helplessness once again as I just held him tighter, resolving in me that nothing and no one can shake me off my will again. To have resistless sight of the profound heights and depths of human nature that were imbued into the depths of Liam's soul, and to be the steady anchor that will light up his winding road from the cave of misery and darkness to see the light.

It seemed that the air was heavily weighted with unasked questions and stifling air that portrayed the melancholy as if it were a mask of unfathomable misunderstanding. Use our artificial intelligence to write for you by entering the text below: Dietary choices can influence the greenhouse gas emissions produced through agricultural practices.

The consumption of meat and dairy products is linked to higher levels of CO_2 The burden of Liam's confession had the same gravity as if it were an invisible blanket, without any escape in sight. Rather than being ready to face reality, the rage detains them, thus the urgency to get some excuse, to find the culprit to ease the pain, to look for the guilty, or to do what to avoid the pain they are feeling inside pops up.

Breathless stutters, hearts thumping, because they were trying to keep count of the waterfall of emotions that poured at them as if it would engulf them, and the writer did a job of mixing that competently. Coming to a climax, the two lost themselves in a passionate game of palms, an interlaced play of fingers that dove deep inside the saddle of their embrace. The emotion of their first struggle illuminated their whole being and was strong enough to leave nothing but the ashes on their skin. They both fight to hide each other's turmoil by diving into their respective rabid fires.

Replacing the studio spaces in the shadows, they left others out, the bodies brushed against each other wildly, and there was aching electricity sliding across the strand of their hair. Deaden whispers in the background that pervade their moans with a gust of loud silence into their aching hearts, wherein lies their deep affliction. The analogy of two souls connected as one and aiming for the least of the comfort they both need to heal the hurt they both felt deep in their hearts best describes their union.

After the tempest had consumed them, they both stopped, their skin expressively reflecting their precious passion. However, the vacuity left behind after the fulfillment of merely carnal Nouns could not be filled with any pleasure, even knowing that the physical commitment had been fulfilled. Their stormy feelings were in need of deeper representation—a surface, a board upon which the struggle between the parts of their disturbed souls could find the expression it deserved.

Feeling the shivers in their hands, they longingly sought their brushes, and their voices were as silent as conspirators in a hushed debate. Sophia's brushwork was sincere, touching, and subtle. The unnamed lady appeared to be tending a ghostly child—a poetic image of the fragile desire burns just faintly in her warmth.

Liam, on the other hand, unleashed his demons with every stroke, his canvas a battleground of abstracted lines and negative space. Each slash of the brush was an exorcism, a purging of the darkness that threatened to consume him. Colors collided in discordant harmony, mirroring the chaos that reigned within his mind.

As the final brushstrokes faded, a profound silence settled upon them, broken only by the soft whispers of their labored breaths. Their eyes met, and in that moment, an unspoken language passed between them—a silent understanding born from the shared experience of laying bare their mottled psyches.

CHAPTER 5

When I approached the gallery, the building's doors had already opened up to me. Such a feeling of ethereal beauty engulfed my soul and my heart. The antiquated white walls shone with tasteful illumination, lending the air a relaxed, luxurious character. My heart beat erratically as a mix of energy and anxiety took over me, watching over my displayed paintings that were meticulously hung and displayed like rare gems on a pedestal.

Suddenly, there was an odd sense of detaching myself from reality that flowed down my spine with the further distance I walked in the gallery. For several months, I'd worked on these paintings, moving me more and more into my personal world of art, closing all the doors and windows, and not paying any attention to anything but the favorite melodies of creativity. It was through every stroke, the use of every color, and the execution of every composition that I tried to translate my deepest feelings. Here they stood, subordinates now, in the shared space, visible to the whole apartment building.

While I was moving around, I could just not make myself hear the crowded, murmuring conversations around me. Owing to the endless conversations among the art critics and connoisseurs of art, I was hearing their voices laden with admiration, curiosity, and fascination. A sense of awe washed over me when I overheard them saying words like "genius," "creative," and "brilliant," like music, which is probably in my ears.

I plowed myself through the crowd of people as my eyes scrutinized the spread, taking a keen interest in the spectators that had come to have a peek at my exhibit. On the walls, I was presented with people who seemed to stand before my paintings, intense and transfixed, much like someone trying to uncover the mysteries woven into all my canvases. Not only do some while others still in an interesting talk shared their different interpretations. Some of them were using gestures in support of their thoughts.

As I listened to their praise and feedback, I felt a warmth spreading through my chest—a sense of pride and validation that I had never experienced before. For so long, I had doubted myself and my abilities, wondering if I truly had what it took to make it as an artist. But now, surrounded by the tangible proof of my dedication and talent, I feel a newfound confidence blossoming within me.

I couldn't help but reflect on the journey that had brought me to this moment. The countless nights spent hunched over my easel, the frustration and self-doubt that had plagued me along the way, the moments of inspiration and breakthrough that had kept me going. It had all been leading up to this, to the realization of my dreams.

As I stood there, taking in the energy and excitement of the room, I felt a sense of gratitude wash over me. I was grateful for the support of my loved ones, for the mentors who had guided me along the way, and for the inner strength that had allowed me to persevere in the face of adversity.

In that moment, surrounded by the fruits of my labor, I felt a sense of purpose and fulfillment that I had never known before. I knew that this was just the beginning and that there were still so many stories to tell and so many emotions to explore through my art. And I was ready to embrace the journey ahead, to continue pouring my heart and soul into each and every painting, and to share my vision with the world.

As I basked in the moment of victory, hysterical from the excessive compliments and admiration at the art show, my eyes suddenly caught a familiar shape immersed in the crowd. And instead, it was my heart that I heard crying out for Liam, my man, who had become irreplaceable and unprecedentedly loyal to everything I was doing as a player. Instantly, a thrill flowed through my body as my eyes locked with hers, and involuntarily, I felt an impish grin creeping on my face.

While Liam was next to me through the hard times as well as the good ones, he has supported me with his own motivational speeches and has always been there to give me a congratulatory hug for my every little victory. It was not simply a matter of 'a partner'; he was so much more to me. He was my trusted confidante, my sounding board, and my most ardent supporter. Besides being here, he has become my dream best-case scenario. Yesterday, I used to pray that I would get that to you, and I was looking at it, intoxicated by gratitude and love.

I parted through the crowd as the crowd I kept humming with my excitement, getting finally to Liam. My enthusiasm for this remarkable accomplishment wouldn't have been complete without him, who shared my joy and delight in such a wonderful moment. I felt like I would hold him close, tell him appreciative words, and notice almost every detail of him as we got this special achievement together.

Yet as I got close, I detected the flashing of something foreign in Liam's eyes—that fleeting instant. The wonting eyes that used to appear while smiling were now substituted with a distressful, rather sad expression. Like a spectral figure haunting him, the darkness took hold of his face, proportionally distorted and greatly different from the happiness and stillness in the air.

I saw a knot in my stomach going deep; it put off my excitement as I got close to her, now that I felt an uneasy feeling. Liam was the one person whose unchanging presence was my bulwark, and, in that instant, he appeared to be totally oblivious to what was happening or as if his mind had been separated from his body.

As I reached out to touch Liam's arm, seeking comfort and reassurance, he suddenly pulled away, as if my touch had burned him. His eyes darted around the room, refusing to meet mine, and I could see the tension in his shoulders, the way his jaw clenched as if he were holding back words that threatened to spill out.

"Sorry, Sophia, I feel I have to go," he said in a mumbling voice, not very audible among the crowds at the art show. My words got choked in my throat, and I was too late to stretch out a hand and question him about the reason of his departure before he powerfully pushed through the row of people.

And I looked, stationary, with my hand still outstretched, while the air itself gave in to my grasp. It is much more stunned than anyone to see the back of Liam's figures fading with the crowd and his broad shoulders and recognizable gait leaving the sights. I was in a ring of wonder as I felt like the world had mysteriously been turned on its side, as I had stepped on a vibration of ground that had unexpectedly revealed itself to be a hole I'd just accidentally fallen in.

But the spark of life that had just lit my heart up seconds earlier, the joy of the evening, and the utmost pride that overcame me then seemed to be nothing more than a brittle shell that was divided by the fact of Liam's sudden leaving. I was confused and hurt—a whirlwind of uncertainties and deep pain. These emotions battled to drown me in their wake.

A barrage of questions was present in my mind, with each coming more heartbreaking than the other. Was it something she had said or done that had made Liam move away so unexpectedly? Did I cause him anger, or was it because of something I said or did that made him upset? Did he keep some unnecessary information, or perhaps a secret, from me?

Oh, how they come close to my eyes. I try to blink them away, as I maybe would say, 'no'. I had been there for a while. Now I simply couldn't. The celebratory mood of everybody who had come to my support to cheer for me destroyed those words, which barely attempted to find their way from my soul to my mind. I weakly took in a breath, trying, to an indefinite extent, to gather strings, reprimanding the emotions that enveloped me inside me like a hard embrace.

But even as I tried to focus on the art show and on the people who still milled around me, congratulating me on my work, I couldn't shake the feeling of unease that had settled in the pit of my stomach. Liam's behavior, his sudden departure, had left me reeling, and I knew that I wouldn't be able to rest until I had answers, until I understood what had driven him away.

The longer the event lasted, the more I looked like an automaton, my smile frozen to my face as I heard myself accustoming myself to the attendees in friendly chats. Their praises and acknowledgments were as soft and far-reaching as ocean waves made out of them, but I was isolated in them by my solitude. My head full of the thoughts of Liam, his unexpected leap out of my mind, twisting and twirling around for the past few moments.

I magnified the critical comments, so the tiny bit of positive feedback only felt like a momentary pleasure. Most of the time, it was like trying to catch a whiff of smoke. When I thought I had escaped to a moment of peace and a sense of completeness, my thoughts would drink a drop of kerosene to create tension in my mind again and again. The deadpan in his eye, the manner in which he had removed himself from me, and the desire in his tone to leave suddenly swirled together like a kaleidoscope out of focus, with the ever-present cloud of confusion and uneasiness.

As the evening wore on, the exhibit pretty much ended; the diminishing trees gradually disappeared. The farther a person walked from the mouth, the quieter the footsteps on the parquet floor became, and then the silence took over, soon to be filled with laughter, chatter, and boisterousness. And, with a well-pronounced terrible, inexplicable feeling, I find myself entirely alone, in the middle of my own painting creation, and I feel the still flow in from every side.

In the absolutely serene atmosphere of the gallery, the apprehension, which had been already throbbing just beneath the skin all evening, eventually overflowed. The imprisonment was almost as if they needed to stretch out their outstretched hand, feeling like that—an awful premonition that I couldn't shake out of my mind. This was a moment of brutal clarity—a truth that I had been desperately trying to avoid, that I had been consciously denying and refuting all along, but now it was lashing out into my face. I had to recognize it.

I stood there, surrounded by the fruits of my labor, the canvases that I had poured my heart and soul into, but they brought me no comfort. Instead, they seemed to mock me, to taunt me with the hollowness of my achievement in the face of Liam's inexplicable behavior.

As I wandered through the gallery, my footsteps echoing in the empty space, I couldn't help but feel a sense of unease, a prickling at the back of my neck that made me feel as though I was being watched. The shadows seemed to lengthen and take on a life of their own, and I found myself jumping at every creak and groan of the old building.

I knew that I couldn't stay here; I couldn't bear to be alone with my thoughts and the growing sense of dread that filled my heart. I needed answers. I needed to understand what had driven Liam away and what secret he was keeping from me.

This morning, the sunrays were proudly popping out through my window, running home to my face with a red Indian tattoo, and quietly awaking me. There was an equally brief period when what had happened in the evening seemed far away from me, like a dream that had never happened. Waking up had been a cathartic moment, and the memories of the very recent events that Liam had left without reason clouded my head. I felt as though a punching bag had hit me on the gut.

My eyes are wide open I went upright on the beach and what was flowing in my veins was something I could not explain anymore but it determined my destiny. We wouldn't be okay with an ending like this; we didn't let Liam get away with such atrocious behavior. I needed to communicate with him to get a sense of what had made him leave and if there was anything I could do to bring about some semblance of the awe-inspiring thing that we had both created!

Fumbling with my hand, I sacrificed my trembling heart to dial Liam's number, my pulse beating like drums through my entire body. Besides the welcoming feeling of his voice, I only heard the machine's voice this time. I was reminded of how indifferent and impersonal a voicemail can be. I had another try, and my fingers were as straight as a race horse, and the output of the numbers was still the same. Voicemail, voicemail, voicemail.

Emotional frustration and anxiety crept into me—a sinking feeling in the bottom of my brain where nothing good could be expected. Liam felt as if simply contacting him would make him disappear. He was not a real person. Only because of that, whenever I allowed my mind to wonder toward dark places, I just tried to imagine all the terrible things that could have happened to him.

Instead, I refused to be taken over by danger and frustration. I did not give up, however, for I was determined to make use of every resource at my disposal while finding a way to communicate with him. I would contact his buddies, his fleet, and any person who might have an idea about his location. I would search everywhere, and I mean everywhere, from every corner of Tbilisi to every place we had ever been together, until I finally found him.

As the days melted into weeks, I found myself caught in a relentless cycle of hope and despair. Every morning, I woke with the desperate expectation that today would be the day I heard from Liam and that he would finally reach out and explain everything. And every night, I went to bed with a heavy heart, the silence of my phone a bitter reminder of his absence.

I was trying to use my art to prevent myself from drowning in the sea of worries. When I did it, I didn't even know how; it was like it had taken on a new life and become someone who was so much stronger than me. I put the hours into my studio, letting my emotions express themselves on the canvas, creating art that was full of emotions that were uncovering my soul and that presented my beauty. It was as if the act of revealing the turbulence going on within me might guard against the darkness from overpowering me.

However, along with the feeling of bliss that came with the act of creation, I was also under the power of a huge fear that ate up all my thoughts. I deeply regret my decision to turn to our mutual friends for help. My friend and I are highly aware of the fact that Liam might be somewhere else, waiting for us. I called anywhere but their numbers, sent the same messages to their inboxes, and begged them for any pieces of information they might have had.

However, the trickle of responses that just kept on coming till the rain poured, all of them disappointments, made me begin to feel more and more disassociated. The last time the family saw Liam, he did not respond to his calls or messages. It was as if he had faded away, disappeared, and was totally gone like never before.

The overwhelming uncertainty was eating me up; I began to confront with questions about disappearance, my very own sanity. An instant fear engulfed me, and I wondered whether everything happened only in my mind. Could I have attributed the Liam character as merely an imaginary thing unreal that was erased by the sunlight of a day?

Nevertheless, this intuition was only deep, and I knew clearly that it was false. It was so unexpected that for a few moments I could still feel the warmth of his touch, still hearing the sound of his laughter. Liam was genuine, and the love we shared was the most real and passionate encounter I had ever had.

Therefore, even though each day passed by without any message or evidence he would return, I held onto this, and it was as though a rope was helping me to hold the fist.

CHAPTER 6

I was in the middle of a crowded art gallery, amidst the buzz of eager guests and the noise of the chinking glasses, but this subtle feeling of uneasiness in my stomach's pit kept on nagging me. When Liam just left the show on a whim, my head was spinning, and I couldn't help feeling as if there was some connection between his vanishing act and the garden.

In this enchanted place, we found the solace, the fountain of creativity, and heartwarming moments, for which we couldn't be more grateful, that all had brought us closer to each other. We had been there a thousand times, making her the space where we did all the talking, the laughing, & the secret sharing. All the time we spent there made it a kind of buoyant bubble for us, where we had a lot of time for dreams & laughter. However, hours after I arrived home, the thoughts of that evening kept visiting me, and instead of the fanciful feeling, I tasted the bitter taste of the truth. The garden was hiding something dark underneath its foliage.

Despite my efforts to move on from that thought, I found myself fixated on the bad news instead of dwelling on the positives of my show and the great receptions of both critics and collectors alike. I do think, however, that by smiling and being grateful to speakers interchangeably, my mind travels to Liam, the man behind my puzzle, instead of the conversations and wishes.

Had I missed something? Was that nervous or awkward behavior, those off-hand comments, anything more than that? I am bothered by my failure to read the warning signs. I couldn't help but remember the times that we had spent together in the garden, where I looked for those small whispers that had been replaced with the gloomy atmosphere hovering above us.

As it was getting late and the night was approaching, I started to make a final decision. I refused to let these virtual feelings take over, and I waited for the end to come. I strangely had to unravel the truth regarding Liam's past and the mysteries that the buried garden revealed.

With a sense of determination burning in my chest, I bid farewell to the remaining guests and slipped out of the gallery. The cool night air hit my face as I stepped outside, but it did little to ease the tension that had settled in my body.

I knew that the path ahead would be difficult and that digging into Liam's past might unearth painful truths and memories. But I also knew that I couldn't turn back now. I loved him too much to let him face his demons alone.

As I made my way home, my mind raced with questions and possibilities. I would start my search in the morning, scouring every source of information I could find. I would piece together the fragments of Liam's history until I had a clear picture of the ghosts that haunted him.

The hidden garden had once been a place of beauty and solace, but now it seemed to hold the key to a mystery that I was determined to solve. No matter how dark the truth might be, I would face it head-on, armed with the strength of my love for Liam and the unwavering belief that together we could overcome any obstacle.

Next to an open window, with the rays of early morning light peeking through it onto my laptop, where I was frantically and thoroughly searching for sources the previous day. The minutes had gone by, not noticeable as I watched the pile of very local and online records, arranging the pieces of Liam's past together.

With every new detail that has been highlighted, and as time went by, a picture that would have been a nightmare was catching my sight. I found out that Liam's family had to leave the garden's property, a mansion that once belonged to the family and passed through generations. The garden was a place with deep roots in their family genealogy—a place where they made their best memories—and the echoes of their laughter would echo through the trees even when strolling alone at late night hours.

However, the deeper I went into the articles' scrapbook, I found a bunch of items that made me jump in horror. Headlines roared that a terrifying calamity happened on the property—something that shook Liam's family beyond the depths of despair and transformed their future into one they could not recognize anymore.

I could almost feel my heart beating out of my chest as I read the description line by line. I could not believe what I was reading—each notch taking me closer to the finale. The fatal accident had brought an end to his parents' lives, which had then made Liam and his siblings orphans and thereby derailed them in a reality that had suddenly turned upside down. This tragedy was caused by the safety rules being neglected, by a carelessness of feeling, and by a simple mistake that resulted in the loss of everything.

While I was reading the articles, I came so close to the truth about Liam's grief, guilt, and the way he had been coping with it all. The heartbreaking moment I was waiting for, that was close to breaking my heart into a million pieces, has finally arrived, and the words on the screen get blurred as I am so engrossed in comprehending the magnitude of the loss.

I've never had the chance to feel what he must have had; I cannot imagine he endures the pain. The sleepless nights he sleeps with the playback of that day chase his mind. The forgotten garden in which they used to play games, like their happiness, faded away from Yeovil forever, becoming just another memory of the event that had destroyed their family.

With every new piece of information, Liam's jigsaw puzzle of the present took on increasingly familiar shapes, finally making him realize that he was an object of his own past ghosts. The mysteries he had kept and the shields he had created to protect himself were understandable yet very enigmatic as the light of such memories poured over him.

Having rested on the back of the chair, my mind was rapidly spinning and brimming with the fallout of the revelation. It was as if I were experiencing Liam's pain personally, and the tears rolling down my face felt so heavy that I could no longer hold them back. At this very instant, I had full conviction that I would go to any extent and perform any act to contribute to his healing and would present to him that he wasn't alone.

I closed down the laptop, and my heart was feeling overwhelmed with the weight of the knowledge. Now onlookers could clearly see the depth of my sorrow lurking around and almost drowning me, but in the midst of that, all I could feel was a tiny spark of resolve. I could be there for him, like a rock, when the hard times come and the paths ahead may be a little murky. The town and the institution would be united in a fight against his demons from the past, and we would learn how to take things one step at a time.

Consequently, in my stubborn manner, I kept hunting for answers as each new nugget of information seemed like a heartbreaker. The trauma that happened to Liam's family was not only a deeper emotional roller coaster, but the devastation was growing inside as well. Every article I read and every detail I found there confirmed that my heart ached for the dear man I love for the suffering he had endured for so long.

I gently leant back into my chair as the tears were coming down my face to try to come as close to realizing what it meant to lose Liam. The support that saved his parents' lives had not only devastated his family but also left a permanent scar on his soul. Indeed, the idea of that man's suffering all these years just for the purpose of giving all of us the chance to live and to be happy pained and saddened me so much.

As a result of it, I started to understand everything in a new way. Liam's hesitation to express himself about his past, his closed-off attitude, and the fortifications that he had erected around his heart have become much clearer now. The secret garden, the spot that had helped her to go through the tragic event that affected his life so much, was not only a beautiful place of comfort, but it was also a place that made me think about those things.

I have been remembering the times we spent together and the fleeting glances of sadness that sometimes appeared to be on his face when he thought that I wasn't paying attention. There was always something within him that he tried to hide, a part of him that had a dark personality, and he tried to keep it at bay as much as he could. Yet I had not visited him in a long time, never prodded, never forced into revelation, wanting to respect his personal space and his pain.

Now, in the light of the emerging truth, I saw what had been going on behind the scenes of my life. It was the unbelievably heavy burden of his loss. Liam has been my shield against that same morbidity that took over him—the sense of dread that shadowed his every moment. The burden he had carried on his own shoulders all this time, unwilling to deface our love with it.

My existence seemed to expand as I eclipsed the earth below—love at the top and sorrow in the middle—a mutually-embracing, bittersweet pain that filled my chest. I pined for an embrace from Liam, for him to hold me close, say words that brought solace, and hear what I was going through. I really felt like I wanted to tell him that he didn't need to be on his own with this pain; I was there, and I would always be next to him each time the wind blew and a storm hit.

When I was there, absorbing his accident details like a sponge, I silently offered myself and him a silent pledge. I would be his balancing pole, his solid surface, which would always stay firm and silent in the whirlwind of his feelings. Together, we will confront those demons that have followed him for years to make him get rid of that guilt so that he can love me.

It was now clear why Liam chose to walk out of the art exhibition during his talk a few months ago. He really came out all this way to freeze me from the morbid anxiety that has been eating him up for so long and to make sure that I wouldn't have to endure the suffering of living with him that he had gone through. Such is the strength of a brother that, no matter how difficult it gets, the brothers stand alongside each other. I would search for him, and together we would hit the road in the shadows until we attained inner strength, which would reflect the light in our love.

I decided to visit the formal garden one afternoon. As I stood there at the entrance of the hidden garden, a rush of emotions hit me like a tidal wave. It was like the once-welcoming gates had taken on a whole new meaning—like they were now a doorway into a world filled with secrets and painful memories. I found myself hesitating, my hand resting on the cool metal latch. I couldn't help but think about how the beauty and peacefulness of this place seemed to clash with the tragic history I had just uncovered.

This garden had been our special place, a sanctuary where Liam and I could find comfort and inspiration. We had spent so many hours here, just wandering along the winding paths, admiring the colorful flowers, and sharing our hopes and dreams with each other. But now, those memories felt bittersweet, tainted by the darkness that I now knew lay beneath the surface.

Taking a deep breath, I stepped inside, the scent of jasmine and honeysuckle filling my lungs. The gravel crunched under my feet as I walked deeper into the garden, each step feeling heavier than the last. The trees and flowers that had once been a comforting presence now seemed to be hiding a painful history, like a beautiful veil concealing the scars of tragedy.

As I walked, my mind was racing with all the things I had discovered. Liam's parents had died in an accident right here, in this very garden. This place that had once brought us so much joy and peace was now forever tied to the most devastating moment of his life. It was like I could feel the weight of his grief and guilt hanging in the air, a tangible presence that seemed to touch every leaf and petal.

I found myself drawn to the bench, where Liam and I had spent countless hours talking and dreaming. Running my fingers along the weathered wood, I traced the patterns in the grain as memories flooded my mind. The laughter, the stolen glances, the gentle touch of his hand against mine—all those precious moments now felt tainted by the knowledge of his pain.

Sitting down on the bench, I closed my eyes and tried to imagine the burden Liam had been carrying all these years. This garden had been a constant reminder of the tragedy that had shattered his world, a living monument to the loss he had suffered. And yet, he had chosen to share this place with me, to let me into his heart and his memories, even as he fought to keep the darkness at bay.

A strange mix of fear and determination settled over me as I sat there, surrounded by both the beauty and the sorrow of the hidden garden. I knew that the road ahead would be tough and that facing the ghosts of Liam's past would take strength and courage from both of us. But I also knew that I was ready to face whatever challenges came our way and to be the rock that Liam needed in this storm.

Opening my eyes, I stood up, looking out over the garden once more. The beauty that had once inspired me now held a deeper meaning, a testament to the resilience of the human spirit and the power of love to heal even the deepest wounds. I knew that together, Liam and I could reclaim this place and transform it from a site of tragedy into a symbol of hope and redemption.

As I sat there on the bench, the weight of Liam's past pressing down on my shoulders, a sudden clarity washed over me. In that moment, amidst the swirling emotions and painful revelations, I knew exactly what I had to do. The path forward became crystal clear in my mind, and a fierce determination took root in my heart.

I had to find Liam. I had to reach out to him, wrap my arms around him, and show him that he didn't have to face his demons alone. For too long, he had carried the burden of his tragedy, shouldering the guilt and grief that had haunted him since that fateful day. But I refused to let him continue to suffer in silence, to let the darkness consume him any longer.

I loved Liam with every fiber of my being, and I was willing to stand by his side, no matter how dark his past might be. I wanted to be his light, his beacon of hope in the midst of the shadows that had engulfed him. I yearned to help him see that he was worthy of love, that his scars and his pain did not define him but rather made him the incredible, resilient man I had fallen for.

With a renewed sense of purpose, I stood up from the bench, my legs trembling slightly as I took a deep breath. I cast one last glance around the hidden garden, taking in the beauty that now seemed to hold a bittersweet essence. This place had brought us together and been the backdrop to our blossoming love, but it had also been the site of Liam's deepest tragedy.

As I walked towards the entrance, I made a silent promise to myself and to Liam. I would not let this garden remain a symbol of pain and loss. Instead, I would help him reclaim it and transform it into a place of healing and redemption. Together, we would create new memories here, ones filled with love, laughter, and the strength of our bond.

Leaving the hidden garden behind, I felt a weight lift from my shoulders, replaced by a fierce determination that propelled me forward. I knew that the road ahead would be challenging and that confronting Liam's past and helping him heal would require patience, understanding, and unwavering love. But I was ready to embark on this journey with him, to be his rock and his shelter in the face of the tempest.

CHAPTER 7

I sat at my kitchen table, my phone in one hand and a pen in the other. I had been calling Liam's close friends and family members for the past hour, hoping to find any information about his whereabouts. With each call, my heart sank a little more as I realized that no one had seen or heard from him recently.

I started with his best friend, Ethan. "I'm sorry, Sophia," he said, his voice laced with concern. "I haven't spoken to Liam in a couple of weeks. The last time we talked, he seemed distant and preoccupied. I asked him if everything was okay, but he just brushed it off."

Next, I called Liam's sister, Olivia. She, too, had noticed a change in her brother's behavior. "He's been withdrawn lately," she confided. "I've tried reaching out to him, but he keeps saying he's fine and just needs some space. I'm worried about him, Sophia."

As I hung up the phone, I felt a growing sense of unease. It wasn't like Liam to just disappear without a word. Something must have happened to push him to this point, and I was determined to find out what it was.

I looked down at the list I had made of the places that were meaningful to Liam. The hidden garden was at the top, followed by his favorite coffee shop and the art gallery where his work had been displayed. I decided to start there, hoping that someone might have seen him or noticed something that could give me a clue about his disappearance.

I grabbed my jacket and keys, my heart racing as I stepped out into the chilly morning air. As I drove to the hidden garden, memories of Liam flooded my mind. I thought of the countless hours we had spent there, talking, laughing, and dreaming about the future. The idea that he might be struggling with something he couldn't share with me made my chest ache.

When I arrived at the garden, I was struck by how empty and lifeless it seemed without Liam by my side. I walked through the winding paths, searching for any sign of him, but found nothing. I sat down on our favorite bench, my eyes filling with tears as I remembered the last time we had been there together.

"Where are you, Liam?" I whispered, my voice trembling. "Please, just let me help you."

I took a deep breath and stood up, brushing away my tears. I knew I couldn't give up. Liam needed me, and I was going to do whatever it took to find him and bring him home.

With a renewed sense of determination, I set off for the coffee shop, hoping that someone there might have seen him. As I walked, I sent up a silent prayer, pleading for the strength and guidance to find the man I loved and help him through whatever darkness he was facing

After leaving the hidden garden, I made my way to the art gallery where Liam's work had been displayed. The familiar scent of paint and canvas greeted me as I stepped inside, and I couldn't help but feel a pang of nostalgia as I remembered the pride on Liam's face during his last exhibition.

I approached the gallery owner, a kind-faced woman named Amelia, and showed her a recent photo of Liam. "Have you seen him lately?" I asked, my voice tinged with hope. "He's been missing for a few days, and I'm trying to find him."

Amelia studied the photo, her brow furrowed in concentration. "I'm sorry, Sophia," she said, shaking her head. "I haven't seen Liam since his last show. He was supposed to drop off some new pieces last week, but he never showed up. I tried calling him, but he didn't answer."

My heart sank at her words, but I forced myself to keep going. "If you hear from him or remember anything that might help, please let me know," I said, handing her my card.

Next, I headed to Liam's favorite coffee shop, a cozy little place where we had spent countless hours talking and dreaming over steaming cups of coffee. I showed Liam's photo to the baristas and regulars, hoping that someone might have seen him.

Most of them shook their heads, offering sympathetic smiles and words of encouragement. But just as I was about to leave, a young barista named Tom approached me. "I saw Liam a few days ago," he said, his voice low. "He came in for his usual order, but he seemed really distracted and preoccupied. I tried to make small talk, but he just mumbled something about needing to figure things out and left in a hurry."

My pulse quickened at his words, and I leaned in closer. "Did he say anything else?" I asked, my voice urgent. "Anything that might give us a clue about where he went?"

Tom thought for a moment, then shook his head. "I'm sorry, that's all I remember," he said. "But if I think of anything else, I'll let you know."

I thanked him and left the coffee shop, my mind racing with this new information. Liam had been there just a few days ago, which meant that he hadn't left town yet. But where could he have gone? What was he trying to figure out?

As I walked back to my car, I couldn't shake the feeling that I was missing something important. I knew Liam better than anyone, and I could tell that he was struggling with something big. But what could it be?

I sat behind the wheel, my eyes closed, as I tried to think. Suddenly, a memory flashed through my mind. Liam had once told me about a place he used to go when he needed to clear his head—a quiet spot by the river where he could sit and think for hours.

My eyes snapped open, and I started the engine. I didn't know if Liam would be there, but it was worth a shot. As I drove, I sent up another silent prayer, hoping that I was on the right track.

With a heavy heart, I drove to Liam's apartment, hoping against hope that he might be there. I had a spare key that he had given me months ago, but I hesitated before using it, not wanting to invade his privacy. I knocked on the door, holding my breath as I waited for a response. But the only sound that greeted me was a deafening silence.

I tried the key, my hand shaking as I unlocked the door and stepped inside. The apartment was dark and still, with no sign of Liam. I flipped on the lights, my eyes scanning the room for any clues that might tell me where he had gone.

As I looked around, I noticed that things seemed slightly out of place. There were dirty dishes in the sink, and a pile of mail had accumulated on the coffee table. It wasn't like Liam to let things go like this.

I walked over to the window, looking out at the city below. That's when I saw Liam's landlord, an older man named Mr. Jameson, walking up the path. I hurried outside to catch him before he went inside.

"Mr. Jameson!" I called out, waving to get his attention. "Can I talk to you for a moment?"

He turned, a look of surprise on his face. "Sophia," he said, nodding in recognition. "What can I do for you?"

I showed him the photo of Liam, my voice trembling as I explained the situation. "Have you seen him lately?" I asked, trying to keep my composure.

Mr. Jameson frowned, his eyes darkening with concern. "Not for a few days," he said. "But he's been acting strange lately. Keeping odd hours, coming and going at all times of the night. I tried to talk to him about it, but he just brushed me off."

I swallowed hard, my worst fears confirmed. "Do you think I could take a look inside his apartment?" I asked, my voice barely above a whisper. "I'm really worried about him."

Mr. Jameson hesitated for a moment, then nodded. "Of course," he said, handing me the master key. "Just let me know if you find anything."

I thanked him and went back inside, my heart racing as I began to search through Liam's things. I looked through his drawers and closets, trying to find any clues that might tell me where he had gone.

As I was about to give up, I noticed a sketchbook lying on his bed. I picked it up, flipping through the pages of beautiful drawings and sketches. But as I neared the end of the book, I stopped short.

There, on the last few pages, were detailed drawings of a remote cabin in the mountains. The sketches were so lifelike that I could almost feel the crisp mountain air on my skin. I studied the drawings closely, trying to make out any identifying features or landmarks.

Suddenly, I remembered a conversation Liam and I had had months ago. He had told me about a cabin his family used to own in the mountains, a place where he had spent countless summers as a child. Could this be the same cabin?

I snapped a photo of the sketches with my phone and hurried out of the apartment, my mind racing with possibilities. I knew I needed to act fast if I was going to find Liam.

As I walked back to my car, I ran into one of Liam's neighbors, a young woman named Sarah. "Hey, Sophia," she said, her face etched with worry. "Have you heard from Liam? He's been acting so strange lately."

I shook my head, my eyes filling with tears. "No, but I think I might know where he is," I said, showing her the photo of the sketches. "I'm going to find him, Sarah. I have to."

She nodded, her eyes wide with understanding. "Good luck," she said, squeezing my hand. "Bring him home safe."

I climbed into my car, my heart pounding in my chest. I knew the road ahead would be long and difficult, but I was ready to face whatever challenges lay ahead. I would find Liam, no matter what it took.

With the sketches of the remote cabin in hand, I knew I needed to take action quickly. As much as I wanted to believe that Liam had simply gone to clear his head, a nagging voice in the back of my mind kept reminding me of the darkness he had been battling.

I made my way to the local police station, my heart pounding with a sense of urgency. As I walked through the doors, I was greeted by a stern-faced officer at the front desk.

"How can I help you, ma'am?" he asked, eyeing me with a mixture of curiosity and concern.

I took a deep breath, steadying myself before speaking. "I need to file a missing person report," I said, my voice wavering slightly. "It's my boyfriend, Liam. He's been gone for a few days, and I'm really worried about him."

The officer nodded, ushering me into a small office where I could provide the details. I showed him the recent photo of Liam and the sketches I had found in his apartment, explaining the circumstances surrounding his disappearance.

"We were planning on going to this cabin in the mountains," I said, pointing to the drawings. "It's a place that holds a lot of meaning for him, and I think he might have gone there to sort things out."

The officer listened intently, jotting down notes as I spoke. When I finished, he looked up at me with a somber expression.

"I understand your concern, Miss," he said, his voice gentle but firm. "But you have to understand that Liam is an adult. If he has chosen to take some time for himself, we can't force him to come back unless there's evidence that he's in danger."

My heart sank at his words, but I refused to give up hope. "Please," I pleaded, tears welling in my eyes. "Liam has been struggling with some personal demons, and I'm afraid he might do something reckless. I just want to make sure he's okay."

The officer regarded me for a moment, his expression softening. "We'll do what we can," he said finally. "But I can't make any promises.

We'll send out a patrol to check the area around the cabin and see if they can locate him."

It wasn't the reassurance I had been hoping for, but it was better than nothing. I thanked the officer and left the station, my mind racing with a thousand different scenarios.

As I walked back to my car, I felt a sense of determination wash over me. If the police couldn't find Liam right away, then I would have to take matters into my own hands. I would go to the cabin myself and search every inch of those mountains until I found him.

I climbed into the driver's seat, pulling up the map on my phone and tracing the route to the remote location. It would be a long journey, but I didn't care. All that mattered was finding Liam and making sure he was safe.

With a renewed sense of determination, I dove headfirst into researching the area surrounding the cabin sketches. I spent countless hours poring over maps, cross-referencing satellite images and topographical data, trying to narrow down the possible locations that matched Liam's drawings.

It was a painstaking process, but I refused to give up. Every detail mattered—the shape of the mountain peaks, the curve of the river, the density of the surrounding forests. I meticulously compared each element to Liam's sketches, searching for any clue that might lead me to his whereabouts.

After days of intense study, I finally identified three potential locations that seemed to align with the drawings. My heart raced with a mixture of excitement and trepidation as I printed out detailed maps and began planning my journey.

I knew this trip would be no easy feat. The cabins were located deep in the heart of the mountains, accessible only by treacherous hiking trails and winding, unpaved roads. But I didn't care. Nothing was going to stop me from finding Liam and bringing him home.

I requested time off from work, citing a family emergency, and packed my gear: sturdy hiking boots, warm layers, a tent, and enough supplies to last for several days in the wilderness. I even invested in a satellite phone, determined to maintain communication no matter how remote my search might take me.

As I loaded my car with the essential equipment, a sense of nervous anticipation settled in the pit of my stomach. This was it—the moment I had been preparing for, the beginning of my quest to find the man I loved.

With one last deep breath, I slid behind the wheel and cranked the engine to life. The familiar rumble of the motor was oddly comforting, a reminder that I was embarking on a journey that would shape the course of my life.

As I pulled out onto the open road, I felt a strange sense of calm wash over me. The uncertainty and fear that had plagued me for days seemed to melt away, replaced by a singular focus: finding Liam, no matter what it took.

The miles ticked by, and the scenery slowly shifted from the familiar cityscape to the rugged beauty of the mountains. Each twist and turn of the road brought me closer to my destination, closer to the answers I so desperately sought.

Finally, as the sun began to dip below the horizon, I reached the outskirts of the search area. I found a small, secluded campground and pulled in, determined to get an early start the following morning.

As I set up my tent and kindled a fire, the weight of my mission settled heavily upon me. I gazed up at the star-studded sky, my thoughts drifting to Liam and the pain he must be enduring.

"I'm coming for you, my love," I whispered into the night, my voice carried away by the gentle breeze. "Just hold on a little longer."

The first rays of dawn found me already on the trail, my backpack weighing heavily on my shoulders as I set out into the rugged wilderness. The crisp mountain air nipped at my cheeks, but I barely noticed; my mind was solely focused on the task at hand: finding Liam's cabin and bringing him home.

For the first few hours, I followed the well-trodden paths, the only sounds being the crunch of my boots on the rocky terrain and the distant call of birds overhead. But as the day wore on, the trails became narrower and less defined, until I found myself blazing my own path through the dense undergrowth.

Sweat beaded on my brow as I pushed forward, my legs burning with exertion. Every so often, I would pause to consult my map and Liam's sketches, searching for any familiar landmarks or geographical features that might point me in the right direction.

As the sun began to dip lower in the sky, I stumbled upon a small cabin nestled in a clearing. Hope surged through me, only to be dashed as I realized it didn't match Liam's drawings. Dejected, I pressed on, determined not to let this minor setback deter me.

Night fell, and I was forced to set up camp, my muscles aching from the day's exertions. As I huddled around the flickering flames of my campfire, I couldn't help but feel a pang of doubt creep into my mind. What if I was on the wrong track? What if I never found the cabin, never found Liam?

I shook my head, banishing the negative thoughts. I couldn't afford to lose faith, not now. With a deep breath, I crawled into my tent and tried to sleep, my dreams haunted by visions of Liam, lost and alone in the vast expanse of the mountains.

The following days blurred together in a haze of sweat and determination. I hiked for hours on end, my feet blistering and my legs trembling with fatigue. Whenever I encountered a fellow hiker or a park ranger, I would show them Liam's photo and the sketches, desperate for any information that might lead me to him.

Most shook their heads, offering sympathetic smiles but no real leads. But then, on the fourth day of my search, I struck gold.

I had stopped to rest by a crystalline stream when a park ranger approached, his face creased with curiosity.

"Excuse me, ma'am," he said, eyeing the sketches in my hand. "Those drawings look awfully familiar. I think I might know the cabin you're looking for."

My heart leapt into my throat as I scrambled to my feet, showing him the sketches with a trembling hand.

"Do you recognize it?" I asked, my voice thick with hope.

The ranger nodded, studying the drawings intently. "Yeah, that's the old Miller place," he said, pointing to a distant peak. "It's a few miles that way, tucked away in a little valley. Mighty hard to find if you don't know where to look."

I could have wept with relief. "Can you show me? Please?"

The ranger must have seen the desperation in my eyes, for he agreed without hesitation. I followed him deeper into the wilderness, my heart pounding in my chest with every step.

Finally, after what felt like an eternity, we crested a ridge, and there it was: a cozy cabin nestled in a verdant valley, its stone chimney puffing smoke into the crisp mountain air. It was an exact match to Liam's drawings, every detail captured with his trademark precision.

Tears stung my eyes as I took in the sight, a sense of relief and trepidation warring within me. I was so close—so tantalizingly close to finding Liam. But what would I find when I reached him? Would he be safe? Would he be happy to see me, or would he push me away once more?

I turned to the ranger, my voice thick with emotion. "Thank you," I said, grasping his hand. "Thank you for leading me here."

He nodded, his expression solemn. "Good luck, miss. I hope you find what you're looking for."

With those parting words, he turned and headed back down the trail, leaving me alone on the ridge, staring down at the cabin that held the answers I had been seeking.

I took a deep breath, steeling my nerves, and began the descent into the valley. Each step brought me closer to Liam, closer to the truth that had driven me to this remote corner of the world.

As I approached the cabin, my heart thundered in my chest, a cacophony of hope and fear. I could see the faint glow of a lamp in the window, a beacon guiding me home.

With a trembling hand, I raised my fist and knocked on the door, holding my breath as the sound echoed through the stillness of the valley.

There was a beat of silence, and then the unmistakable sound of footsteps approaching from within.

The door creaked open, and there he was—Liam, his eyes wide with disbelief and a ghost of a smile playing on his lips.

"Sophia," he whispered, his voice barely audible. "You found me."

In that moment, every ounce of fear and doubt melted away, replaced by a rush of pure love and relief. I stepped forward, wrapping my arms around him and pulling him close, tears streaming down my face.

As Liam and I embraced on the porch of the remote cabin, a torrent of emotions washed over me. Relief at finally finding him, concern for his well-being, love for the man who held my heart—it was a maelstrom of feelings that threatened to overwhelm me.

Pulling back, I searched his face, taking in the dark circles under his eyes and the haunted look that seemed to have taken up permanent residence in his gaze. My heart ached for him, for the pain he had been carrying alone all this time.

"Liam," I whispered, my voice trembling. "Why didn't you tell me? Why did you run away?"

He averted his eyes, shame and guilt etched into the lines of his face. "I couldn't bear the thought of you seeing me like this," he murmured. "Seeing the darkness that consumes me."

I cupped his cheek gently, turning his face back towards me. "Don't you understand?" I said, my eyes shining with unshed tears. "Your darkness is not something to be afraid of. Not when I'm here to share the burden with you."

Liam shook his head, a bitter laugh escaping his lips. "You don't know the half of it, Sophia. The things I've done, the guilt that weighs on my soul... He trailed off, his voice thick with anguish.

Gently, I took his hand and led him to the porch swing, settling down beside him. The cool mountain air caressed our faces as we sat in silence, the weight of unspoken truths hanging between us.

Finally, Liam took a deep breath and began to speak. "Do you remember when I told you about the accident that claimed my parents' lives?" he asked, his voice barely above a whisper.

I nodded, my heart clenching at the memory.

"What I didn't tell you," he continued, "was that it was my fault."

The words hung in the air, heavy and damning. I stared at him, my mouth agape, as he unraveled the painful tale.

It had been a stupid mistake, he explained, a moment of carelessness that had led to an unimaginable tragedy. His parents had been on their way to pick him up from an art competition when their car collided with a drunk driver, ending their lives in an instant.

"If I hadn't been so selfish, so wrapped up in my own ambitions, they would still be alive."

Liam choked out, his shoulders shaking with barely contained sobs. "It's my fault they're gone, Sophia. And I've been carrying that guilt with me every single day."

In that moment, my heart shattered for him. I had always known that Liam's past was shrouded in pain, but I had never imagined the depths of his suffering. Without a second thought, I pulled him into my arms, holding him as he wept, his tears soaking into the fabric of my shirt.

"Oh, Liam," I murmured, stroking his hair gently. "You've been carrying this burden for far too long."

As his sobs subsided, I tilted his chin up, looking into his eyes with a fierce determination. "What happened to your parents was a tragedy, but it wasn't your fault," I said, my voice firm yet gentle. "You were just a child, Liam. You couldn't have known; you couldn't have prevented what happened."

He opened his mouth to protest, but I pressed on, refusing to let him wallow in self-blame any longer.

"Your parents wouldn't want you to live like this, consumed by guilt and pain," I said. "They would want you to find happiness and to live your life to the fullest."

Liam fell silent, his eyes searching mine for any hint of deception or pity. But all he found was love—unwavering and true.

Slowly, hesitantly, he began to nod, his shoulders sagging with a weight that had finally been lifted. "You're right," he whispered, his voice hoarse from crying. "I've been holding onto this for far too long."

We sat there on the porch swing, wrapped in each other's embrace, as the sun dipped below the mountains. In the fading light, I could see the glimmer of hope in Liam's eyes, a spark that had been dimmed by years of guilt and pain.

It would be a long road ahead, a journey filled with challenges and setbacks. But in that moment, I knew that we would face them together, our love a beacon guiding us through the darkness and into the light.

With a tender kiss pressed to his forehead, I made a silent vow to Liam and to myself: we would heal, one step at a time, and emerge stronger than ever before. The path would be difficult, but with our hearts entwined, we would find our way home.

CHAPTER 8

The crackling of the fire was the only sound that filled the cozy cabin as Liam and I sat on the worn sofa, our hands intertwined. The weight of the silence was almost palpable, but I knew better than to rush him. After all this time and all the pain he had bottled up inside, he needed to open up at his own pace.

Liam took a deep, steady breath, his eyes fixed on the dancing flames. "I was ten years old when it happened," he began, his voice barely above a whisper. "My parents were on their way to pick me up from an art competition, one I had been so excited for."

He paused, swallowing hard as the memories washed over him. "I can still remember the pride in their voices when they called earlier that day, telling me how much they were looking forward to seeing my work. They were my biggest supporters, my whole world."

A single tear rolled down his cheek, and I squeezed his hand gently, offering what little comfort I could.

"The accident happened so quickly," Liam continued, his voice trembling. "One moment, they were on their way, and the next..." He trailed off, the unspoken words hanging heavy in the air.

I shifted closer, wrapping my arm around his shoulders as he leaned into me, seeking solace in my embrace.

"From the moment I got the news, something inside me broke," he whispered, his eyes glazed with unshed tears. "I was just a child, but I felt this overwhelming sense of responsibility, like it was my fault they were gone."

The pain in his voice was palpable, and I ached to take it all away, to erase the years of guilt and anguish that had weighed him down.

"I tried to move on, to be strong for my siblings," he said. "But the guilt never went away. It was a constant companion, a shadow that followed me everywhere I went."

Liam turned to me then, his eyes searching mine for understanding. "I know it sounds irrational, but that fear, that sense of responsibility, kept me from truly healing. I was afraid to let go, afraid to forgive myself."

In that moment, I saw the depth of his suffering—the years of torment that had carved lines into his soul. Without a word, I pulled him closer, holding him as he finally allowed the tears to flow freely.

We sat like that for what felt like an eternity, the only sounds being his muffled sobs and the steady crackle of the fire. And as I held him, I made a silent vow—I would be his strength, his anchor in the storm that had raged within him for far too long.

When his tears finally subsided, Liam pulled away, his eyes red-rimmed but filled with a newfound vulnerability.

"Thank you," he whispered, his voice rough with emotion. "For being here, for listening."

I cupped his face in my hand, my heart swelling with love and determination. "Always," I promised. "No matter what, I'll always be here for you."

As Liam's words faded into silence, I could feel the weight of his pain hanging in the air, thick and suffocating. My heart ached for him, for the little boy who had shouldered a burden far too heavy for his young shoulders.

I reached out, gently brushing away the tears that lingered on his cheeks. "Liam, my love," I murmured, my voice thick with emotion. "What happened to your parents was a tragedy, but it was not your fault."

He opened his mouth to protest, but I pressed on, unwilling to let him continue down the path of self-blame and guilt.

"You were just a child," I said, my eyes locked on his. "You couldn't have known; you couldn't have prevented what happened. The only ones responsible were the drunk driver and the cruel twist of fate."

Liam's gaze dropped, his shoulders sagging as if the weight of years had suddenly settled upon him once more.

"But I felt so responsible," he whispered, his voice barely audible. "If I hadn't been so focused on that stupid art competition, if I hadn't been so selfish..."

"Stop," I said firmly, reaching out to grasp his hand in mine. "Stop punishing yourself for being a child and for having dreams and ambitions."

I gave his hand a gentle squeeze, my heart swelling with a fierce determination to help him see the truth.

"Your parents loved you, Liam. They loved your passion for art and your boundless creativity. They wouldn't want you to live with this guilt and this pain. They would want you to be happy, to find joy in the life they sacrificed so much to give you."

Tears welled in Liam's eyes as he listened to my words, his defenses slowly crumbling under the weight of my unwavering love and support.

"But how?" he asked, his voice breaking. "How do I let go of something that has been a part of me for so long?"

I reached out, cupping his cheek in my palm and offering him a tender smile. "One day at a time, my love. One moment, one breath at a time."

I pulled him into my embrace, holding him close as the gentle rise and fall of his chest matched the steady beat of my own heart.

"I know it won't be easy," I murmured into his ear. "But you don't have to face this alone anymore. I'm here, and I'm not going anywhere."

Liam melted into my arms, his body trembling with the release of long-held tension and grief.

"Thank you," he whispered, his words muffled against my shoulder. "Thank you for seeing me and for loving me despite my brokenness."

I pressed a soft kiss to the top of his head, my heart swelling with a love so profound that it threatened to consume me.

"Always," I promised, holding him tighter. "I will always see you, Liam. And I will always love you, no matter what."

In that moment, something shifted between us—a bond forged in the fires of pain and resilience. We had taken the first step on a journey that would test our strength, our love, and our commitment to one another

The days that followed were a whirlwind of emotions—a constant ebb and flow between hope and despair. Despite my reassurances and unwavering love, I could see the struggle within Liam—the battle raging between his desire to heal and the guilt that had become a part of his very essence.

We spent our days exploring the beauty of the mountains, hiking through lush forests, and basking in the serenity of crystal-clear lakes. It was during these moments of solitude that Liam seemed to find a fleeting sense of peace, his shoulders relaxing as he lost himself in the majesty of nature.

But as the sun dipped below the horizon, casting long shadows across the valley, the demons would return. I would watch helplessly as Liam retreated into himself, his eyes haunted by memories that refused to fade.

One evening, as we sat by the crackling fire, the tension between us became palpable. Liam fidgeted restlessly, his gaze fixed on the dancing flames.

"I'm trying," he whispered, his voice strained. "Believe me, Sophia, I'm trying to let go."

I reached out, covering his hand with my own and offering what little comfort I could.

"I know you are," I murmured, my heart aching for his suffering.

Liam shook his head, his eyes glistening with unshed tears. "But it's like this weight, this anchor, that keeps dragging me down. No matter how hard I try to break free, it just"

His voice trailed off, and he buried his face in his hand, his shoulders shaking with silent sobs.

In that moment, I saw the depth of his anguish—the years of guilt and self-loathing that had carved their way into his very soul. Without hesitation, I pulled him into my arms, holding him as he finally allowed the floodgates to open.

"Why can't I forgive myself?" He cried, his words muffled against my shoulder. "Why can't I just let it go?"

I tightened my embrace, rocking him gently as his tears soaked into the fabric of my shirt.

"Because you've been carrying this burden for so long," I whispered, my own eyes stinging with tears. "It's become a part of you, a part of your identity."

Liam lifted his head, his eyes red-rimmed and filled with a pain that cut me to the core.

"But I'm so tired, Sophia," he rasped, his voice thick with emotion. "I'm tired of living in the shadows, of letting this guilt consume me."

I cupped his face in my hand, my gaze unwavering as I stared into the depths of his haunted eyes.

"Then let me be your light, my love," I said, my voice steady despite the tremors that coursed through my body. "Let me guide you out of the darkness and into the warmth of love and acceptance."

Liam searched my face, his expression a complicated mix of longing and fear, as if he were teetering on the edge of a precipice, terrified to take that final leap.

"Or, what if I can't?" He whispered, his voice laced with doubt. "What if I'm not worthy of love, or happiness?"

In that moment, my heart swelled with a fierce determination, a resolve that burned brighter than the flames that danced before us.

"You are worthy," I stated, my words ringing with conviction. "You are worthy of love, of joy, and of a life free from the shackles of guilt and pain."

I pulled him close once more, my lips grazing his forehead in a tender kiss.

"And I will spend every day reminding you of that truth, until the shadows have been banished and you can bask in the light that you so deserve."

As I held him, I could feel the tension begin to seep from his body, the weight of years slowly lifting from his shoulders. It would be a long and arduous journey, but in that moment, I knew that we had taken the first step towards healing, towards a future where love and forgiveness would triumph over the demons of the past.

As we sat together one morning, sipping coffee on the porch of the cozy cabin, I broached the idea that had been forming in my mind.

"Liam," I began, my voice gentle yet resolute. "I think it's time we paid a visit to the places from your childhood."

He tensed beside me, his knuckles whitening as he gripped his mug tighter.

"I'm not sure I'm ready for that," he murmured, his gaze fixed on the distant peaks.

I reached out, covering his hand with my own and offering a reassuring squeeze.

"I know it won't be easy," I said, my voice laced with understanding. "But confronting the past and revisiting those memories might be the key to unlocking the healing you so desperately crave."

Liam was silent for a long moment, his brow furrowed as he wrestled with the weight of my suggestion. Finally, he turned to me, his eyes shimmering with a mix of fear and determination.

"Alright," he said, his voice barely above a whisper. "Let's do it."

The journey to his hometown was a somber one, with each mile marker a reminder of the ghosts that haunted our path. But as the familiar streets and landmarks came into view, I could see a flicker of recognition in Liam's eyes, a spark of nostalgia that ignited despite the weight of his sorrow.

We began our tour at the park where he had spent countless hours as a child, chasing butterflies and climbing trees with reckless abandon. Liam pointed out the old oak where he had carved his initials, a wistful smile tugging at the corners of his mouth.

Next, we visited the elementary school he had attended, wandering the halls that had once echoed with the laughter and shouts of carefree youth. Liam paused before a display case, his fingers tracing the outline of a faded photograph—a cherished memory captured in time, forever frozen in the innocence of childhood.

As the day wore on, we visited one haunt after another, each location a portal into Liam's past. With every stop, he seemed to shed a little more of the burden he had carried for so long, his shoulders straightening and his steps growing lighter.

It was at the local diner, the one his parents had frequented, that the floodgates finally opened. As we slid into the worn vinyl booth, the familiar scent of greasy fries and fresh-brewed coffee wafting around us, Liam's eyes misted over with tears.

"They used to bring me here every Sunday after church," he whispered, his voice thick with emotion. "Mom would always order the same thing—a stack of pancakes with extra syrup and a side of crispy bacon."

A melancholic smile curled his lips as he lost himself in the memory, his fingers tracing invisible patterns on the tabletop.

"Dad would tease her about her sweet tooth, but she didn't care. She loved those pancakes; she loved the way the syrup would run down her chin and make her laugh like a little kid."

I reached across the table, covering his hand with my own as he spoke, offering a tether to the present even as he revisited the ghosts of his past.

For hours, we lingered in that diner, Liam regaling me with stories of his parents, their quirks and their love, their unwavering support, and their boundless joy. With each tale, I could see the weight lifting from his shoulders, the shadows retreating ever so slightly, until the man before me was bathed in the warm glow of cherished memories.

As the sun began to dip below the horizon, casting the town in a golden hue, we made our way back to the car, our hearts full and our spirits lighter than they had been in weeks.

Liam paused before sliding into the passenger seat, his eyes finding mine in the fading light.

"Thank you," he murmured, his voice laced with a depth of emotion that stole my breath away. "Thank you for pushing me to confront the past and for helping me see that it's not all pain and sorrow."

I stepped forward, cradling his face in my hand, my thumbs brushing away the tears that lingered on his cheeks.

"You don't have to thank me, my love," I whispered, offering him a tender smile. "This is just the beginning. Together, we'll continue to chase the light until the darkness has been banished for good."

On the way back to our cabin with the towering mountains behind us, I was grateful and confident that we had accomplished something big and that our path to healing had commenced. The road ahead remains tortuous, and there will still be obstacles, but for the first time in a long while, a bit of light can be seen through the darkness of Liam's knightly outfit.

As our trip down memory lane drew to a close, there was one final destination that loomed before us: a place that held the power to either shatter Liam's newfound peace or cement the foundation of his healing. With heavy hearts and trembling hands, we made our way to the cemetery, where Liam's parents had been laid to rest.

The drive was silent, and the air was thick with a mix of trepidation and resolve. I could see the tension in Liam's jaw, the way his knuckles whitened as he gripped the steering wheel, but there was a determination in his eyes that hadn't been there before, a flicker of courage that refused to be extinguished.

As we stepped through the wrought-iron gates, the gravel crunching beneath our feet, Liam's steps faltered. I reached out, lacing my fingers through his, offering a silent reminder that he wasn't alone and that I would be there every step of the way.

We wound our way through the rows of headstones, the names and dates blurring together, until we reached the one that bore the names of Liam's parents. Liam froze, his breath catching in his throat as he stared at the granite marker, the weight of years crashing down upon him in that moment.

Slowly, hesitantly, he sank to his knees, his fingers tracing the engraved letters that spelled out the names of the two people he had loved and lost so tragically. I stood back, giving him the space he needed to confront the ghosts that had haunted him for so long.

For a long moment, Liam was silent, his shoulders shaking with the force of his emotions. And then, like a dam finally bursting, the tears began to flow, a torrent of grief and guilt and long-suppressed anguish pouring out of him in waves.

"I'm sorry," he whispered, his voice raw and broken. "I'm so sorry for blaming myself and for holding onto the guilt for so long."

He bowed his head, his tears falling like rain onto the grass that blanketed his parents' final resting place.

"I know now that it wasn't my fault," he continued, his words punctuated by sobs. "I know that you would want me to be happy and to live my life without the weight of this burden."

As he spoke, I could feel my own tears streaming down my face, my heart aching for the man I loved and the pain he had endured for so long. But there was something else there too: a flicker of hope, a sense that this moment, as raw and painful as it was, marked a turning point in Liam's journey towards healing.

Slowly, I approached him, sinking to my knees beside him and wrapping my arms around his trembling frame. He leaned into me, his head coming to rest on my shoulder as he wept, the years of pent-up emotion pouring out of him in a cathartic release.

We stayed like that for what felt like hours, with the sun dipping below the horizon and casting the cemetery in a soft, ethereal glow. And as Liam's tears began to subside, I felt a shift in the air—a sense of something heavy and oppressive finally lifting from his shoulders.

When he finally pulled back, his eyes were red-rimmed but clear, a peace settling over his features that I had never seen before. He reached out, cupping my face in his hand, his thumb brushing away the tears that lingered on my cheeks.

"Thank you," he whispered, his voice hoarse but steady. "Thank you for being here and for helping me find the strength to let go."

I leaned into his touch, my heart swelling with a love so profound that it stole my breath away.

"You did this, Liam," I murmured, my eyes locked on his. "You found the courage to confront your past, to release the guilt and the pain. I was just lucky enough to be here to witness it."

He smiled then, a real, genuine smile that lit up his entire face, and in that moment, I knew that we had turned a corner. The road ahead would still be long and winding, but Liam had taken a monumental step towards healing, towards freeing himself from the shackles of his past.

As we rose to our feet, hand in hand, I could feel the change in Liam's energy, the lightness in his step, and the hope in his eyes. He paused, casting one last glance at his parents' headstone, a silent promise passing between them.

"I love you," he whispered, his words carried away on the evening breeze. "And I promise to live my life in a way that would make you proud."

With that, we turned and made our way out of the cemetery, the weight of the past finally beginning to lift from our shoulders. The future stretched out before us, a blank canvas waiting to be painted with the colors of our love and the hope of a brighter tomorrow.

We had left the mountains behind, the cabin and the memories it held fading into the distance like a half-remembered dream. But the changes that had taken place there—the steps we had taken towards healing and forgiveness, were etched into our hearts, a permanent reminder of the journey we had embarked upon together.

As we navigated the busy streets, the familiar sights and sounds of the city enveloping us like a comforting embrace, Liam turned to me, his eyes sparkling with a newfound sense of purpose.

"Let's start over," he said, his voice filled with determination. "Let's create a space that represents our new beginning, a place where we can build a future together."

I felt my heart swell with love and excitement; the idea of starting anew with Liam filled me with a sense of hope and possibility.

"I think that's a wonderful idea," I replied, my hand finding his and giving it a gentle squeeze. "We can renovate your apartment or find a new place altogether. Whatever feels right for us."

Liam nodded, his smile widening as he lost himself in thought. I could almost see the gears turning in his head and the plans and ideas taking shape as we drove.

Over the next few weeks, we threw ourselves into the process of creating our new home. We spent hours poring over interior design magazines, browsing furniture stores, and debating color schemes. Liam's artistic eye and my practical sensibilities made for an interesting combination, but somehow, we always managed to find a compromise that felt right for both of us.

As the days turned into weeks, our new space began to take shape. We had decided to start fresh, finding a cozy apartment in a vibrant neighborhood that felt like the perfect blend of our personalities.

Slowly but surely, we filled it with pieces that held meaning for us—a painting Liam had created during our trip to the mountains, a set of vintage books we had discovered at a quaint little shop, a collection of photographs that chronicled our journey together.

With each new addition, our apartment began to feel more and more like home, a reflection of the love and resilience that had brought us to this point. And as we stood together in the center of our new living room, surrounded by the tangible reminders of our bond, I could feel a sense of peace and contentment settling over us like a warm blanket.

Liam pulled me into his arms, his chin resting on the top of my head as we swayed gently to the rhythm of our own heartbeats. In that moment, I knew that we had weathered the storm and that the trials and tribulations we had faced had only served to strengthen our love and deepen our connection.

"Thank you," Liam murmured, his breath tickling my ear. "Thank you for never giving up on me, for loving me through the darkness and guiding me back into the light."

I tilted my head up, my eyes meeting his, a smile curving my lips.

"You never gave up on yourself, my love," I replied, my hand coming up to caress his cheek. "You found the strength to confront your past, to let go of the guilt and the pain. I was just lucky enough to be by your side through it all."

Liam leaned down, capturing my lips in a tender kiss that held the promise of a lifetime. As we lost ourselves in the moment, the world falling away until there was nothing but the two of us, I could feel the excitement and hope of our new beginning thrumming through every fiber of my being.

We had emerged from the darkness, battered but unbroken, our love a beacon guiding us into the future. And as we stood there, wrapped in each other's arms, I knew that whatever challenges lay ahead, we would face them together, our bond unbreakable and our hearts forever intertwined.

This was our new beginning, a chapter waiting to be written, and I couldn't wait to see what the future held. With Liam by my side, I knew that anything was possible and that our love could conquer any obstacle and weather any storm.

CHAPTER 9

I awoke to the gentle caress of the morning sun on my face, its warmth seeping into my skin like a tender embrace. As I slowly opened my eyes, blinking away the last vestiges of sleep, I felt a sudden rush of energy surging through my body, a sensation I hadn't experienced in what felt like an eternity.

Beside me, Liam lay sleeping, his features soft and relaxed, a stark contrast to the haunted expression that had once seemed etched into his very being. I propped myself up on one elbow, taking a moment to drink in the sight of him and marveling at the peace that had settled over him in the weeks since our return from the mountains.

Our journey had been a long and arduous one, filled with moments of gut-wrenching pain and heart-wrenching revelations. But through it all, our love had been a constant, a guiding light that had led us out of the darkness and into the warmth of a new dawn.

As I watched Liam sleep, his chest rising and falling with the steady rhythm of his dreams, I felt a sudden surge of inspiration wash over me, a feeling so powerful that it nearly took my breath away. In that moment, I realized that our story, the love we shared, and the healing we had undergone together had given me a profound new perspective on life and art.

My mind raced with images and ideas, snippets of our journey flashing before my eyes like a film reel. I thought back to the countless paintings I had created over the years, each one a reflection of my own emotions and experiences. But now, armed with the clarity of hindsight and the wisdom gained from our trials, I see my art in a new light.

I slipped out of bed, careful not to disturb Liam's peaceful slumber. I tiptoed into the living room, my bare feet sinking into the plush carpet as my mind buzzed with a frenzy of inspiration. I could see it so clearly in my mind's eye—a painting that would capture the essence of our story, a testament to the power of love and the resilience of the human spirit.

The urge to create was overwhelming—a wild and untamed force that demanded to be given form. It was as if every moment of our journey, every tear shed, and every triumph celebrated had been leading me to this point, to this singular act of creation.

I gathered my art supplies with a trembling hand, pulling out a fresh canvas and an array of paints and brushes. I set up my easel by the window, allowing the golden light of the morning to spill across the pristine surface before me.

For a moment, I simply stood there, my heart pounding with a heady mix of excitement and trepidation. I knew, with a certainty that rang through every fiber of my being, that the painting I was about to create would be my most meaningful yet—a reflection of the love and the healing that had transformed our lives.

With a deep breath, I picked up my brush, dipping it into the vibrant hues that seemed to call out to me, their colors singing a siren's song of emotion and meaning. As I set the bristles to the canvas, I could feel the emotions welling up inside me—a torrent of love, gratitude, and hope that flowed through me like a raging river, guiding my hand as I began to paint.

In that moment, the world fell away, and there was nothing but the canvas, the story that burned within me, and the love that had brought us to this point. I lost myself in the act of creation, pouring my heart and soul into every brushstroke, every line and curve, and every splash of color.

I painted our love the way it had blossomed like a rose in the midst of the darkest night. I painted our pain—the shadows that had threatened to consume us, only to be banished by the radiant light of our bond. And I painted our future—the endless possibilities that stretched out before us, a blank canvas waiting to be filled with the colors of our dreams.

As the morning wore on, the painting began to take shape, a beautiful and haunting testament to the power of love and the indomitable nature of the human spirit. And as I stepped back to admire my work, I felt a sense of peace and purpose settle over me, a deep knowing that this was what I was meant to do - to share our story with the world and inspire others to find hope and healing, even in the face of the greatest challenges.

With a renewed sense of purpose, I set up my easel in the living room, the soft light filtering through the windows casting a gentle glow on the blank canvas before me. I could feel the anticipation thrumming through my veins as I began to sketch out the ideas that had been swirling in my mind, the rough lines and shapes slowly taking form on the pristine surface.

As I worked, I found myself lost in the memories of our journey, each stroke of the pencil bringing to life a different moment and a different emotion. I sketched the winding path that had led us to the hidden garden, the place where our love had first blossomed like a delicate flower. I drew the majestic mountains that had borne witness to Liam's deepest pain, their jagged peaks and deep valleys mirroring the scars that had once marred his heart.

But amidst the shadows and the sorrow, I also sketched the moments of triumph, the small victories that had lit our way like stars in the night sky. I drew the tender embrace we had shared after Liam's breakthrough—the way our hearts had beaten as one in the stillness of the mountain air. I sketched the gentle curve of his smile and the way his eyes had sparkled with newfound hope and love.

As I stepped back to examine my work, I felt a presence behind me. Turning, I saw Liam standing in the doorway, his eyes wide with wonder as he took in the rough composition that had begun to take shape on the canvas.

"Sophia," he breathed, his voice soft with awe. "This is incredible."

I felt a flush of pride and love warm my cheeks as I met his gaze, seeing the admiration and support shining in his eyes. Liam crossed the room to stand beside me, his arm slipping around my waist as he studied the sketch more closely.

"I want to capture our story," I explained, leaning into his embrace. "Every struggle, every triumph, every moment that brought us to where we are now."

Liam nodded, his fingers tracing the lines of the sketch with a reverent touch. "It's perfect," he murmured. "A testament to the power of our love and the strength of our bond."

With Liam's encouragement and support, I felt a renewed sense of passion and purpose flood through me. I knew that the painting I was about to create would be more than just a work of art; it would be a reflection of our souls, a mirror held up to the love that had saved us both.

As I began to paint, I found myself drawn to the colors that seemed to whisper the story of our journey. I reached for the warm, vibrant hues first—the rich reds and oranges that spoke of the passion and love that had been our guiding light, even in the darkest of times.

I painted the fiery glow of the sunrise over the mountains, the way it had cast a golden halo around Liam's figure as he stood on the porch of the cabin, his eyes closed in a moment of quiet contemplation. I used the warm, honeyed tones of the wooden beams that had sheltered us—the way they seemed to absorb the love and laughter that had filled the air.

But as I worked, I also found myself reaching for the cooler, more muted shades—the colors that seemed to whisper of the pain and sorrow we had endured. I painted the deep blues of the night sky, the inky darkness that had once threatened to swallow us whole. I used the pale grays and silvers of the mist that had clung to the mountains, the way it had mirrored the veil of grief that had once shrouded Liam's heart.

And yet, even amidst the shadows and the sorrow, I found myself weaving in hints of brightness, small flashes of color that spoke of the hope and healing that had slowly begun to take root. I painted the delicate pinks and purples of the wildflowers that had bloomed in the hidden garden; the way they had seemed to symbolize the fragile beauty of our love. I used the soft greens of the forest and the way the leaves danced in the breeze like a whispered promise of new beginnings.

As I stepped back to survey my work, I felt a sense of awe wash over me. The colors on the canvas seemed to sing with emotion, each hue and shade telling a story of its own. And yet, when woven together, they created a tapestry of love and resilience, a testament to the journey Liam and I had taken and the bond we had forged in the fire of our shared pain.

I felt Liam's presence beside me once more, his hand coming to rest on the small of my back as he gazed at the painting with misty eyes.

"It's beautiful," he whispered, his voice thick with emotion. "You've captured it all—the love, the pain, the hope. It's like looking into the very heart of our story."

I leaned into his touch, my own eyes brimming with tears of gratitude and love. I knew that the painting was far from finished and that there were still countless details and nuances to be added. But in that moment, I felt a sense of deep satisfaction, a knowledge that I was creating something that would endure long after Liam and I were gone, a testament to the power of love to heal even the deepest wounds.

In the days following the completion of my painting, Liam and I found ourselves lost in long, heartfelt conversations about our future together. We sat for hours on the couch, our hands intertwined, as we poured out our hopes, dreams, and fears, laying bare the very essence of our souls.

As we talked, I couldn't help but marvel at the depth of the bond we had forged and the way our love had been tested and tempered in the crucible of our shared pain. We had faced challenges that would have broken lesser relationships; we had stared into the abyss of grief and despair and come out the other side stronger and more united than ever before. and

Liam's eyes sparkled with a newfound clarity as he spoke of his hopes for our future, his voice filled with a quiet conviction that took my breath away. "Sophia," he said, his fingers tracing the delicate lines of my palm. "I know that the road ahead won't always be easy. Life has a way of throwing curveballs when we least expect them. But I also know that with you by my side, there's nothing we can't overcome."

I felt my heart swell with love and gratitude as I gazed into his eyes, seeing the unwavering devotion and commitment that shone within their depths. "You're right," I murmured, bringing his hand to my lips and pressing a soft kiss to his knuckles. "We've already weathered so many storms together. And each one has only made us stronger and more resilient."

In that moment, a sense of profound peace and certainty settled over us, a deep knowing that our love was the foundation upon which we would build our future. We made a promise to each other then, a vow that we would face whatever challenges lay ahead as a team, united by the unbreakable bond of our love and the hard-won wisdom of our shared journey.

As we sealed our promise with a kiss, I felt a sense of excitement and anticipation coursing through my veins. I knew that our path forward wouldn't always be smooth and that there would be obstacles and setbacks along the way. But I also knew that with Liam by my side, I could face anything, secure in the knowledge that our love would be our guiding light and our north star in even the darkest of nights.

In the weeks that followed, as Liam and I began to plan for our future together, I found myself increasingly drawn to the idea of sharing my painting with the world. The more I thought about it, the more I became convinced that our story had the power to inspire others and to offer hope and comfort to those who were struggling with their own pain and grief.

I broached the idea with Liam one evening as we sat on the balcony of our apartment, watching the sunset paint the sky in shades of gold and pink. "I want to have a small gallery showing," I said, my voice soft but filled with conviction. "Just for our friends and family, to start. But eventually, I'd like to share our story with a wider audience, to let others know that even in the darkest of times, there is always hope."

Liam's eyes shone with pride and admiration as he pulled me close, his lips brushing against my temple in a tender kiss. "I think that's a wonderful idea," he murmured. "Your painting is a testament to the power of love and resilience, a reminder that beauty can be found even in the midst of great sorrow. If it can bring comfort to even one person who is struggling, then it will have served its purpose."

And so, with Liam's support and encouragement, I began to plan for the unveiling of my painting. I reached out to our closest friends and family, inviting them to a small, intimate gathering at a local gallery space. I spent long hours carefully selecting the perfect frame and the perfect lighting, wanting every detail to be just right.

When the day of the unveiling finally arrived, I felt a flutter of nerves in the pit of my stomach as I stood beside Liam, my hand clasped tightly in his. The gallery was filled with the soft murmur of conversation, the air thick with anticipation as our loved ones gathered around the veiled painting.

As I stepped forward to address the room, I felt Liam's reassuring presence beside me and his love and support as a tangible force that buoyed me up and gave me strength. "Thank you all for coming," I began, my voice trembling slightly with emotion. "The painting you're about to see is more than just a work of art to me. It's a reflection of the journey Liam and I have taken together, a testament to the power of love to heal even the deepest wounds."

With a deep breath, I reached out and grasped the edge of the veil, slowly pulling it back to reveal the painting beneath. As the fabric fell away, a collective gasp filled the room, followed by a reverent silence that seemed to stretch on for an eternity.

There, on the canvas, was the story of our love, rendered in vibrant hues and delicate brushstrokes. The painting, titled "Love's Healing Embrace," was a swirling tapestry of color and emotion, each element carefully chosen to evoke the essence of our journey.

In the center of the canvas, two figures stood locked in a tender embrace, their bodies intertwined in a dance of love and devotion. Around them, the landscape shifted and changed, from the dark, shadowy hues of the mountains to the warm, golden glow of the hidden garden. And woven throughout it all were symbols of hope and renewal—delicate wildflowers blooming in the cracks of a broken boulder, a single ray of sunlight piercing through a veil of mist.

And as I gazed into the faces of my loved ones—the sparkle in those tearful eyes and those beamers of pure happiness on their mouths—a sense of relationship joy washed all over me. At the moment, I felt a sheer satisfaction in knowing that my work had reached its goal, that is, namely, had turned into a symbol of hope and aspiration for all those who ever looked at it.

He extended his arms and pulled me into his open embrace. Tears were running down his face, and I cherished the instant when I felt overwhelmed with a sense of gratitude for having undergone such a great path. Our story, written down in the colors of our lives, had become the most prominent picture of the human spirit, showing the way, presenting purity and joy, even amid pain and suffering.

With life around me filling the room with a light but audible murmur of conversation again and more people, among them our friends and family, coming forward to congratulate us and express gratitude, I leaned into Liam's arms, my heart, so full of love and joy. I realized that this course of ours was more than just the views from the window; it had things more challenging and triumphs as well. But I also remembered that we had love to help us, that we had learned strength and wisdom together, and that there was nothing else we had to face since the road we had common tread.

CHAPTER 10

It's hard to believe that it's been five years since Liam and I first found each other in the hidden garden. So much has changed since then, but one thing remains constant: the love and bond we share. As I walk hand in hand with him through the winding paths of the garden, I can't help but feel overwhelmed with gratitude for the journey we've been on together.

The sun is setting, casting a warm glow over the flowers and trees that have become so familiar to us. It's like the garden is wrapping us in a comforting embrace, reminding us of the healing and growth we've experienced here. I lean into Liam, feeling his solid presence beside me, and I know that I'm exactly where I'm meant to be.

Life hasn't always been easy, of course. We've faced our fair share of challenges and obstacles over the years. But through it all, our love has been the one constant, the guiding light that's helped us navigate even the darkest of times. And now, as we run our own art gallery together, I feel like we've truly found our calling.

It's funny to think back on how hesitant I was when that first gallery approached me about showcasing my work. I was so unsure of myself, so afraid to take that leap. But Liam believed in me, just like he always has, and with his encouragement, I found the courage to put myself out there. And now, seeing my art on the walls of our own gallery, knowing that it has the power to touch and inspire others—it's a feeling I can hardly describe.

Liam has grown so much too, both as an artist and as a person. Watching him come into his own, seeing the way his talent and passion shine through in every piece he creates, fills me with a sense of pride and awe. He's not just my partner in life, but in art too, and I know that together, we can achieve anything we set our minds to.

But even with all the success and joy we've found, we never forget the lessons we learned on our journey to healing. That's why we make sure to come back to the hidden garden as often as we can to soak in the peace and beauty of this special place. It's a reminder to slow down, to appreciate the simple things, and to never take our love for granted.

As we walk, I can't help but marvel at the twists and turns that brought us here. The hidden garden was the catalyst for so much change—the place where our broken pieces started to come together again. It's seen our tears and our laughter, our pain and our joy. And now, it feels like an old friend, a silent witness to the love story we've written together.

Liam squeezes my hand, pulling me close to him. "I love you, Sophia," he murmurs, his voice soft and full of emotion. "I love our life, our gallery, and the way you make every day an adventure. You're my everything."

Tears spring to my eyes as I look up at him, my heart so full it feels like it might burst. "I love you too, Liam," I whisper back. "More than words can say. You're my rock, my soulmate, and my partner in every way. I thank the universe every day for bringing you into my life."

We stand there for a long moment, wrapped in each other's arms, as the last light of day fades into a starry night sky. I know that our story is far from over and that there will be plenty more ups and downs in the years to come. But I also know that as long as we have each other and as long as we hold onto the love and lessons we've learned, there's nothing we can't face.

Because, in the end, that's the real magic of the hidden garden. It's not just a physical place, but a symbol of the transformative power of love and human connection. It's a reminder that even in our darkest moments, there is always hope, and beauty to be found. And as Liam and I walk back to our gallery, hand in hand, I know that we'll carry that message with us wherever we go, sharing it with the world through our art and our love.

Life is an adventure, full of twists and turns and unexpected detours. But with Liam by my side, I know that every step of the journey will be worth it. Because together, we've found the kind of love that legends are made of. The kind of love that heals, inspires, and transforms. The kind of love that lasts a lifetime.

About the Author

Lila Vex is an emerging talent in the world of romance literature, captivating readers with her tales of love and adventure. With her skillful storytelling and vibrant characters, she transports readers to enchanting worlds where love conquers all.

When she's not immersed in writing her next romance novel, Lila enjoys exploring the great outdoors and indulging in her love for travel.

Stay updated on Lila Vex's latest releases and projects by visiting her website.

Read more at https://www.lilavex.com/.

www.ingramcontent.com/pod-product-compliance
Lightning Source LLC
Chambersburg PA
CBHW020617130626
46552CB00003B/1011